A Witch's Wand

breaking up with a possessed battery-operated boyfriend

April Klasen

Independently Published
2024

First Printing: 2024

Paperback ISBN 978-1-923217-99-7
E-book ISBN 978-1-923217-98-0

April Klasen
aprilklasenauthor@hotmail.com

Acknowledgements

Thanks to my best friend for inspiring me yet again. This would never exist without you, **Caitlin**. And I love you.

But I swear to God if you jinxed me with your message, "This is going to be your defining work." I will curse you to always step on Lego at 3am.

And thanks to **Mother** for being forced to proofread my paper copies. It had to be done. Just, don't think too hard about what you read.

Content Warning

Hi there,

A Witch's Wand started off as a joke, but quickly became something a lot darker than intended. This is not going to be a story for all readers.

And that's okay.

Please be mindful of your mental health and if you need help, you are not alone. **Ask for help.**

A Witch's Wand contains:

- Occult themes
- Millennial humour including jokes about suicide
- Non consent to voyeurism
- Sexual harassment and assault
- Unhealthy coping mechanisms
- Explicit sex scenes

But it does have a happy ending. Heather does get her shit together and makes it to the other side of all of this.

Like all of my stories, this is a safe space to explore ideas and fantasies. What happens in the imagination does not necessarily mean that it is desired in real life. But this is where we can explore and consider and learn and heal.

Happy Reading!
April Klasen

I should get up. I should get up.
I should get up and do something.
Make dinner. Stretch. Clean. Get up and do anything as long as it is something more than… this. Come on Heather. Get. UP!

I scrolled through another round of videos served up by the algorithm that knew my habits so well. I scrolled and felt nothing.

Travel videos. Exotic destinations. Bright colours. The creators all wearing the same long flowy dresses as they show off how amazing their lives are.

Finance videos. Tips on how to save and grow money. Normally, from someone who was already making seven figures and they made these videos telling people how they too could be like them, just sign up for their e-course, on sale for a limited time.

Cat videos.

Gym videos.

Funny videos.

Book reviews.

Thirst traps.

I watched them all. Hardly blinking as I flicked my thumb over the screen moving to the next one. And the next one. And the one after that.

The same audio used for three in a row. Then a throwback to an audio popular two years ago. Back to another with the same sound.

I scrolled onto another book review. Instead of it being one of the fan faves everyone was raving about, some of which I had on my ever-growing TBR, this one was… different.

"What the…" I turned the volume up to listen to the reviewer. It was not young adult fantasy. No dystopian vibes. No enemies to lovers.

No.

"It's a fucking erotic romance about a Pinocchio," I cackled to myself.

Of course, the reviewer did not call it that. They described how this lonely piece of furniture, a chair, had loved her always and been watching over her as it sat in her bedroom. And wished to have the chance to be a real man and to take care of her… in all ways a man could.

"He wants to be a real boy!" I snorted. "A real boy so he could bang her. Ugh. Why are even men in fiction like those in real life? They all just want to get their dicks wet."

I scrolled away.

But how does he become real?

I scrolled back and suffered through watching the beginning explanation once more. Then… "Oh!" my eyes went wide at the description. Not graphic. Of course not. The app would not allow such vulgar things.

No. Instead, it was a little sentence. "She had spicey time on the chair and magic took that and made him into a man."

What a ridiculous explanation, I thought. All the while still wondering what kind of spicey times? Was it chair humping? Was it inserting a chair leg? Something else?

"And the reviews," the content creator continued talking fast. "Are all saying this is a good read. That it is more than another sentient object erotic romance. It has soul. I give this read a solid 4 chair legs out of 5."

I pondered for a moment before leaving the app. *I'll have a look. If it's a ridiculous price, I won't touch it… but if it's like, not bad, or even free… No harm. Plus, it's supporting an author,* I rationalised.

It wasn't free.

But it was within my book budget. It was the usual price I paid when I wanted to read something… not that I could remember… "When did I last pick up a book?" I lowered my phone to my chest and frowned.

No answer to that question.

I tried to remember when I last touched a book and read instead of, well, doom scroll. It was probably when I bought that handful of 'must reads' that had been… less than impressive. Unfortunately. *Back at the start of the year?*

"I should read more," I said as I clicked purchase of this random story. "I should take a book with me to read during my lunch break at work. I really should do that."

Even as I said this, I stayed reclined on my lounge, switching from the browser to the reading app and seeing the book make its way into my library.

I didn't go and pick a paperback from my TBR pile and stick it into my work bag. Ignoring the fact I needed to take that same bag to the kitchen and get my lunch box out, do the prep for tomorrow's work day so I wasn't frazzled and racing around in the morning to get ready and be out the door on time.

Nope. Not me. Not Heather. Instead, I started to read this new book and ignored everything else in my life.

"Wow." I read something fun and flirty. An author who knew their audience well had penned this. I liked that. Liked that the writing was something easy for me to read. It even made the fact the love interest was a damn chair sound so natural. Nothing about it so far was jarring me out of the story.

"This is pretty good," I admitted aloud.

Then came the spice.

"Oh my," I gasped as I read the words of what the female main character was doing. "That's... ohhhh. Hmmm," I bit my lip. *Holy shit!* She was going all out.

My guesses had been incorrect. The MC wasn't humping or inserting parts of the chair into herself.

"That's an honest to god dildo that she has there," I announced. There was no reason to do so. I was the only one in the house. The only one listening. But talking to myself wasn't weird. *Was it?*

The MC had a dildo, one with a suction end, and went over to smack that down onto the chair. Of course, I had to say something. Who wouldn't be vocal about something like that?!

I also had to fan my face a little. "My oh my. What an interesting idea."

I read;

She took the dildo into hand and gave it a sharp tug, ensuring the suction cup held firm to the seat of the chair. It didn't budge. She smirked a little. Good, she needed it to be firmly in place for what she wanted to do with it.

Looking over her shoulder, as if she feared someone to be there but finding her room empty, she turned around. Her face burned. Was she doing this? Had she become so desperate for cock that she was about to bounce on a rubber imitation and imagine that it was a real one?

She spread her legs and reached between to hold the shaft as she lowered herself. Its unfamiliar head touched her and she shuddered. "Oh God," she bit her lip. God, she wanted this so bad. Wanted to have something filling her up.

She ached.

Rolling her hips, she teased herself, heated the head up. It slid through her wet lips. Nudged her throbbing clit a couple of times. Then she guided it back to where she needed it. Its head, a section that bulged out, pushed in as she lowered. Stretched her.

She moaned as it did.

Once she passed that, the rest slid in easily with gravity getting her down. And then she was seated. Her ass cheeks pressed to the wood of the chair and dildo

shoved so deep inside she whimpered. "Ugh… fuck… me," she gripped onto the arms of the chair to steady herself. It was good. So good. Oh hell, she rocked a little and the toy shifted inside.

Tentatively, she rose up. Hovered so that the head was still inside but was back to stretching her opening, and then dropped. Slammed herself back down. It jarred hard inside of her. She repeated. And again. And again. A lift and lower and it felt like she was slamming down onto a real dick.

But it wasn't easy to do that. Her legs ached. Shook with the controlled effort. And though there was pleasure in getting jackhammered like that at first, it did hurt after a while.

If only she was being nailed by someone real, then she could let them take over. Could lean back into them and whisper how much she loved having their cock filling her up. Beg them to cum inside. Taunt them until they would call her a dirty whore, their dirty little whore, and hold her in place and fucked up into her.

But she was alone. She had to put in the work to get herself off. Typical.

She released her grip on the chair. Ran her fingertips over her waist and dragged them up to her breasts. Both palms cupping, squeezing and stroking, pinching her nipples and tugging on them to feel a similar tug in her clit every time she did.

She leant forward as she started to lift and lower. It was still not right and took so much effort! She hated letting her breasts go to place her hands in her knees, giving her more stability. Arched her back as she lifted.

Lost in it all, she didn't realise… the change.

The chair, the one that had sat in the corner of her bedroom and watched her everyday as she dressed, had started to transform. It had been sentient for a while now and wished it could've done more than hold the clothes she threw onto it. It was getting it's wish.

Suddenly, he touched her.

An arm wrapped around her waist and hauled her back until she collided with a solid chest. Another hand came up to begin groping her breast.

She started. "Wha?!" What was happening?! Who the hell was this that was… was doing her?!

But her panic failed to take over as the cock inside of her moved on its own. It was thrusting up, hard and fast and hitting all of her spots deep inside. She was overwhelmed. Threw her head back and moaned.

"That's my girl," a deep voice rumbled by her ear.

Who was fucking her?!

She had been all alone in her room when she'd started and hadn't lifted off of the dildo once, so no-one could've slipped in and under her.

And yet… there was someone else. A man. Who held her in place with an arm about her waist and was driving into her relentlessly.

She panted hard.

His lips grazed over her neck, making her shiver and roll her head to the side to give him better access.

She whimpered when teeth sunk in and bit, followed by tongue lapping over the mark, and lips kissing it better.

She was insane. Who the hell ignored the sudden appearance of a man in favour for getting railed by him? Her, apparently.

"Please," she begged.

"Please what?"

She frowned. What did she want? She didn't have the capacity to think in specifics, not with how rough he was being.

"Hmm?" he prompted. "Do you want me to slow down?"

She shook her head violently at that suggestion. "Noooo," she whined.

He chuckled. "Do you want me to touch you?" he released her breast and dragged his hand down to brush it over her clit.

She moaned at the contact. But also shook her head.

"No?" he asked. "But you sounded like you enjoyed my fingers there."

"Please... hmmm, please, sir." She gasped.

"Do you want to cum?"

Her head bounced hard. Yes. Yes! That's what she wanted. Needed. She wanted to cum. "Please, please, please."

"Be a good girl for me and cum on my cock," he ordered. He then pressed hard onto her clit with the base of his palm. Every thrust up of his hips jolted her forward onto his hand and dragged her clit over it.

It built hard and then… and then.

"Ahhhh," she screamed. Clenched around his dick. Spine arched. Head thrown back onto his shoulder. Nails digging into his forearm.

He slowed his thrusts until they were gentle rocks inside of her… and then he lowered her.

She gasped at being sat directly onto the dildo once more while she was coming down from the intensity of her orgasm.

Again, she didn't notice the change.

It took a moment for her to regain clarity and to swivel her head to look at whom it was who had screwed her… only to find no-one. She was sitting on the chair, dildo in her pussy, and no man to be seen.

"But…" she trailed off. Was she going insane? Had she'd been drugged and hallucinated it all? Or was she losing her mind?!

She still felt the achy throb in her neck… "Oh!" she surged up. Regretted it immediately as the dildo's length dragged through her and out. Had to take a moment to catch herself with her hands on the end of the bed, bent over and ass pointed at the chair.

Once stable again, she went to her mirror and found exactly what she'd needed. Her proof. A love bite. Fresh, with indents from teeth, darkening into a bruise.

She spun around to her chair and stared.

It was a plain piece of furniture. Toy standing tall on it's seat, covered in all of the juices from her pussy.

"What the fuck?" she murmured to herself. "What the fuck was that?"

I bit my lip and ached after reading that scene. Jesus.

Who thought of this shit? What kind of pervert did you have to be to think of something like this, write it, and then publish it for the whole world to read? And then what kind of deviant was I for thinking this was one of the hottest things I'd read in a while? For wanting this to happen to me… hmm?

Yep, that was the motivation I needed.

I surged up and off of the lounge and hurried towards my bedroom. Eager.

I stripped off every item of clothing I had and discarded it all to the floor without care. Detoured to the bedside table, to the top drawer. Inside nestled the collection of toys. *Which one today? Which one did I feel like using?*

This empty feeling made the choice easier. I ached to have something inside of me, like the main character of that story. I needed it. But my clit also throbbed, wanting attention desperately.

I picked.

A vibrator in the classic sense, but the added bonus of a clit sucker that did exactly what the title implied. It was a smooth design. A sleek dildo, five inches at most and not girthy at all. It was a perfect fit for me. Was comfortable, *ha, yes "comfortable."* A good size to have inside and to do myself on.

Emerging from the side in this graceful arc was the part that came up and covered the clitoris. That was one element I would have changed, because it sometimes didn't stay in position, would go off to the side. Awful! A horrible thing to have happen right when I desperately needed direct contact. It should've been bigger. More surface area.

But I didn't design the thing.

If I had I would've made the handle for it follow the same curve as the clit sucker, made it more ergonomic for me to use on myself. Unfortunately, the handle was in line with the dildo. Meant reaching further down to have a decent grip on it to hit the right angles if I was thrusting it in and out. As is, it made me wonder if they had designed it to look sleek. Or if it was designed for it to be used on me and not for me to use on myself.

I could imagine another person holding it. Grasping the handle with a sure hand and pushing it in, going deep, the clit sucker hitting the bundle of nerves. Then pulling back to repeat it all again.

Hmmm. Fuck. Biting my lip, I had to clench my thighs as I throbbed to do that. Just that.

No point in waiting, I dropped onto the bed and adjusted so my head laid across the pillow and legs spread out. Wide.

I dragged the vibrator head through my labia, lubed it up with the wet mess I'd become from reading. *I was this wet from a written description?! Bloody Hell. How shameless.* Brought the tip up to my clit and rubbed it around. Got it wet.

Then slipped it back down and pressed in. Shallow. Brief. To feel that stretch around it. Just the tip. I pushed and pulled it until I wanted, needed, more. That's when I slid it all in on one move and gasped. "Fuuuu… hmmm."

I fought hard to keep my thighs apart, to dig my heels into the mattress and have them wide. But my knees tipped and ugh, if only I had someone there. Someone my thighs could close around and squeeze. Hook my legs over their hips and try to draw them in deeper.

I pumped it a few times, making sure the entire length was wet and gliding effortlessly. Each press forward brought the clit sucker into direct contact with my clitoris. Pressed on it.

I could do this. Fuck it in and out and enjoy the friction. Bloody hell, it would get me to cum. But always after a while and always after my wrist and forearm cramped and switching it to my non-dominant hand interrupted the flow. I wasn't as steady and sure with it. Couldn't hit directly the same way or maintain the same pace.

Or…

I pushed the length all the way in, adjusted so the clit sucker sat over it with clear contact… and turned the vibration on.

Now, my thighs clamped together. Gripped the handle in place for me.

I pressed the buttons and drove the fluttering vibrations on my clit higher and higher. Chose a simple repetitive pattern for the dildo, so it vibrated and felt a little like someone was nailing me, even if the shaft stayed in place.

There. Oh shit. There.

The vibrations were working on my body hard. Making it feel so damn good.

I dragged my hands back up. Skimmed them over my hips and waist. Scooped my breasts and massaged them. My finger pads rubbed over my nipples, made them harden and stand out. I touched all over.

One palm released and went high. Collar bones. Throat. Finally, lips. I traced the bottom lip, tongue poking out to wet the tip of the digit, help it glide easier.

I wanted to be kissed.

I wanted to press my lips against someone else's skin and trail them all over.

I wanted to have them close around body parts.

It's ridiculous how I still ached for something… *no, forget that. Focus on what you're doing, Heather. Or make it into a fantasy. Yeah, make it into a fantasy person who has a dick fucked up inside of you. And… and a second one feeding their cock into your mouth.*

I pushed my fingers in and sucked on them. Moaned around them. God, it was hot.

My hips rocked on their own.

I was getting closer. Soon. But I wanted it now. I needed to cum now!

Taking my fingers from my mouth, I brought them to the handle. Just the tips of two, positioned on the end… I pushed. It rocked the vibrator in. Released. Pushed again. Over and over. I fucked it in gentle rocks. *A tap, tap.* Each more solid press against my clit helped to hurry me along. *Tap, tap, tap!* It became more frenzied.

Come on, come on, please, I need it.

It hit hard. A wave of pleasure that crashed over me, gave me full body shivers. I screamed. Tried to muffle it with a hurried hand over my mouth. *Fuck. Fuck me. Oh damn it!*

It felt amazing.

Pulling the still buzzing vibrator out, made me shudder at how over stimulating that was.

A mess covered the entire shaft. My body ached and throbbed, felt glad to have been used as such.

I chuckled, blissed out of my body, and flopped back, toy still in hand to keep from spreading the mess all over my sheets. Turned it off.

That had been… yeah, that had been yeah ha ha ha… I grinned like a fool at my ceiling.

A good way to spend an evening.

Silence echoed, in that odd way that it does when alone. Especially, in the dark.

"I don't want a boyfriend," I told myself firmly. Because of course that's where my brain goes immediately after an orgasm. But… the house was empty. And I… damn it. I didn't like how it made me feel.

I started to reach out for my phone, only to realise two things. First, the vibrator was still in my grasp. Second, my phone was in the lounge room.

"Oops," I grimaced. No jumping online to distract myself quickly before I let my thoughts wander too far away.

Not that I should be controlling my mind like it's a toddler needing supervision and distraction. It's just… no. I don't want to think about it.

It's a simple fact, I am not interested in settling for some guy because I… I'm… no! I am not settling.

Angry at myself, I hauled my ass off of the bed and stalked to the bathroom. The toy needed to be cleaned. That's all. It's a necessary task.

Under the water, I rinsed off the worst of the mess and used some soap to clean it. Rubbing my palm all over it, dipping the tip of my finger into the little suction section and making sure to get all the areas. Then turned the water to scalding hot and held the vibe underneath it.

"I am happy being single," I repeated to myself. "The best I've ever had has been from battery-operated devices." A strange thing to admit.

The fact I preferred an inanimate object to a real, breathing human being with a personality and hopes and dreams… and opinions, expectations, the emotional intelligence of a rock. "Ha… maybe there isn't so much difference after all."

The only difference being that I could reach an orgasm with it rather than any of my past experiences with men.

I'm bitter.

No, I chastised myself. *I expected life to be… to turn out…*

"Ugh! Come on, Heather," I looked up at the mirror, met my gaze and tried to hold it. But couldn't. Damn it, when did I become such a coward? I looked away and gritted my teeth.

What did I want my life to be?

This?

Or something else?

"Really am… I am happy I'm single. That's not a lie." This time, I was able to hold my gaze in the mirror. "I don't need anyone… I just," my mouth pulled into a grimace. "If only my vibrator could be like a Pinocchio and become a real man. Battery-operated boyfriend. He'd be perfect," I snorted. "Could get me off in record time, be a presence in the house so it's not so empty, snuggles. Oh, I miss snuggles."

When was the last time I had touched another human?

I don't remember even the last time I had a hug or… or… holy shit, I can't honestly be counting into years, can I?

I turned off the stream of water and shook off the excess from the vibe. "You are the closest thing to a long-term relationship I've ever had," I admitted to the object.

No word of a lie.

I placed it carefully onto the stack of towels to air dry and washed my own hands.

But the idea kind of stuck. A battery-operated boyfriend. I didn't want all of the other things that came from having a romantic partner. But it would be nice to come home to someone. To have them put my pleasure first, to prioritise my needs in the bedroom.

Of course, in those books, the ones where he was an object and wished to be alive, it was fiction. I'm not delusional enough to think that making a wish on a star was going to bring an object to life. To begin with, most of them were sentient from the start and the coming to life was taking it from a weird thing to being acceptable.

Who wanted to admit they had a relationship with a chair? No-one! It was more normal to say I sit on my boyfriend like a chair.

Buuuuut… "Huh, that's an idea."

What if I could make my vibrator into something with a conscience?

I turned off the tap and glanced at the vibe in question.

It was both a silly idea, but also one with a very interesting and very real possibility. After all, there were things out there that science had yet to catch up to quantifying and theorising.

Things only witchcraft and spirituality had made sense of.

I took one step, heading to the door, then paused. "Oh yeah." My thighs were sticky. And other places felt… icky. I needed to clean up.

I huffed a sigh and jumped into the shower. All, while still letting my head spin away with this ridiculous concept. *Yes, this could work. Or it could fail and nothing happens. Either way, what was the risk?*

The box sat at the top of a cupboard. Put away years ago with no clue whether to keep everything, burn it, or toss it out. What was I going to do, come back to the craft after not practicing for a few years? Was that even allowed?

"At least I still have something here to look through," I admitted under my breath. Once safely down from the stool I took the box to the coffee table, sat on the floor myself, and popped the lid.

"Oh, I forgot about those!" I cried out in honest surprise. My little jars were still in their packaging. So cute and so tiny! I never did feel like making a spell jar. Not a spell jar for money or love or protection. None of those resonated with me. But I'd bought them anyway. And kept them.

It was an odd collection of things. A jar filled with old nails, coins, and pebbles. Oracle cards. Tarot deck. Some crystals, even though I didn't feel like they were for me, but every witch blog insisted that I needed at least some selenite to cleanse everything.

What was that black one called again?

And why do I have so much rose quartz? Was I trying to amass enough to summon a whole harem of potential lovers?

My spell book sat at the bottom. I flipped through. Marvelled at the intricate pages I'd made, with proper calligraphy and little ink sketches filling in the empty spaces.

And then those pages ended. I hadn't done more than five. They were beautiful. And I remembered how frustrating they were to plan out and to make perfect.

"Why was I being so careful though? It's not like I was planning on ever sharing this book with anyone." I closed it up when I saw it was the same old boring beginner stuff. The things we're all told to research first before any other spells. The history of the craft, protections, cleansing… not what I wanted.

No, I wanted something else.

A little further down, under it all was just the thing. A teabag.

Yep. My one most magical thing was a humble teabag. And it had been the first thing I had been able to use properly.

"Why didn't I grab one from the kitchen," I frowned. "I didn't have to pull this box out if I only needed this. Stupid, Heather." I scolded myself.

But I wasn't sure if I wouldn't find something in there and have a sudden 'aha!' moment. So yeah, I guess there was a reason. More than nostalgia.

I leant forward and placed my elbow onto the table top. The tag of the string pinched between my fingers letting the bag hang and swing freely.

Taking a deep breath, I lowered the teabag to rest on the table with me. Eyes closed. Breathe out. Focus on stilling my mind.

Deep breath in, and raised my hand again, making sure I remained steady and not influencing the swing of the tea-bag. I released my breath. "Show me a yes," I asked.

It moved, swinging back and forward in a very clear answer.

"Show me a no," I asked.

It changed to swing side to side.

My elbow was braced, so I wasn't shaking. No window was opened. Even if no-one else believed or they scoffed at this idea, I was convinced that I was using the pendulum correctly.

"Um…" and I was using it to ask such a silly question! *Oh my God, what am I doing?!*

I sighed.

"Can I invite a willing spirit or entity or something to possess my vibrator?" Words left my mouth. My face burned. It sounded worse out loud. I groaned and watched the teabag easily swing back and forth in a yes.

Ah! Okay, that um… well.

"Thank you for your guidance!" I yelled at the teabag and lowered it back to the tabletop before dropping it completely and covering my face.

I inhaled deep and then bemoaned what I'd asked. Toppled sideways to sprawl over the floor. "Whhhhhyyyyy? Why did I ask the Universe that question? It's so ridiculous. Ugh, I'm a loser."

A loser who was still thinking of how it would be to have a sentient vibe, one that I could talk to…

"Talk to a vibrator?" *I need to get a hold of myself. No, enough for the night. It is late and I have another torturous shift at work tomorrow. Yay me.*

With a drawn-out groan, I hauled myself up and headed to bed.

Couldn't sleep after ten minutes. "I'll watch something online," I said. Reached for my phone plugged into my charger and brought it over. The bright illumination of the screen hurt my eyes.

When I unlocked... it was still on the page for the book. Still right where I'd finished reading to run off and masturbate. Where the MC was trying to process what had happened and the possibility that her chair had come to life and shagged her.

Again, I knew this was fiction. No amount of wanting was going to cause a full transformation from silicone into a living and breathing man. Not to mention the absolute size difference... *as a body, not dick size!* There wouldn't be enough of anything to have the equivalent exchange of energy to make something bigger.

No, in reality, what I could do, if it worked out, would be to invite something to take up residence and make it sentient.

That's all.

And again, that would probably be the best sort of boyfriend.

No fights, because what are you fighting over? Orgasms since it's still a vibrator. And the presence of someone there so I didn't feel so damn alone all the time.

"I would need to put in parameters," I lowered the phone and started to list off on my fingers what I needed. How I would word things to make sure I was not inviting anything bad into my life.

"No bad boys," I told myself sternly. "Only those who mean me no harm and are willing. Yeah, that sounds like a good combo."

I smiled to myself as I imagined what it was going to be like.

If it works.

But if it did, I would be a bloody genius! I would have the best boyfriend. I would be spending an entire week in bed screwing myself with them. Hell, if it's that good I could even see if more wanted to possess my other toys. *Ha! Have my own little harem living in my top drawer. All for my pleasure exclusively.*

I giggled at that. Kicked my feet under the covers as I imagined the weird little harem. The possibilities of what could happen. Like if I used more than one toy at a time, would they be jealous or work well together or be competitive.

"Ugh, come on Heather!" I chastised. "You haven't even gotten this to work for one, let alone your whole collection. Just be cool and see what happens. Tomorrow. Need to sleep now, to work in the am, and then you can play all witchy and see what happens." I popped the phone back on the charger and rolled over, cuddling my pillow.

*

"Okay," I took a deep cleansing breath. "Show time."

I sat in the middle of the bed, legs crossed. In front of me, the vibrator was presented. I'd even stopped by the grocery store on the way home and snagged a rose bouquet so I could scatter the petals around. Really add to the ambiance. And possibly mean something to all of this, you know, red roses for passion and sex. Maybe it would help attract the right entity.

I too, may have dressed for the occasion. Dragged out my old lingerie from the bottom of my knicker drawer and dolled myself up to match it; hair in a loose wave, perfume.

I felt… sexy. I liked what I looked like in the mirror, but it was how I was feeling. How I felt like I was desirable. How I felt like I wanted someone to see me like this, to want me, to touch me.

I let my hands drift over my body in appreciation. Skimmed over the edges of the lace panties and around to feel my ass, cup each cheek and marvel at how amazing it was. *I have a great ass.*

Then trailed fingers up my waist and to the bra. *Dear god, that's what my tits looked like when I wore something proper.* Cleavage. A lot of cleavage. I played with it. Cheekily poking the soft flesh and then properly gripping and squeezing to feel how nice it was. Like when I touched my butt.

Hmm. I liked that a lot. Almost to the point of wanting to use the toy on the bed as is. *Slip my panties to the side and hmmm… No. I dressed for a purpose!* And that was to try something unusual. I didn't put it on for myself.

And if this didn't work, it'll be a waste of my effort. I'd probably crawl into some comfy oversized pyjamas and hibernate. Burn the lingerie.

Hush, focus time.

My eyes closed.

This wasn't going to be a chanting of a spell and wait and see. No this was going to involve a bit more effort on my part.

Slowly, I allowed myself to go into a meditation. Breathed deep and clear. Mind empty. *Let go. Let go. Let it all go.* I exhaled each time and yeah, it worked.

Feeling calm, I brought my focus to visualising my bedroom. Only it wasn't the one I was in. It was my dream bedroom, the one I would have if I could. A massive princess four poster bed with sheer curtains draped over the canopy and down the sides. Mountains of pillows. Dark green wallpaper. All of the furniture in dark wood. Hardwood floors with a lush rug to step my toes onto in the morning.

In front of me was the same vibrator. But now it sat on top of it's very own little golden pillow.

"I invite someone willing, who means me no harm, to take possession of this… device," I shared the words in the visualisation.

When I looked up from the vibrator, I saw a figure standing at the foot of the bed. A blue man. He grinned at me.

"Do you mean me harm?"

He shook his head, still smiling.

It was unnerving. Or maybe it was because I hadn't visualised him. This was… an entity. Something else.

He was blue. Like primary colour of blue. Huge hulking man.

"Do you know what this is? What it's used for?"

This time, he nodded his head.

My face burned. *Was I going to do this? To invite him in and… hold on! He was blue. Oh no, does this make me a Smurf fucker?*

He stared at me. Not blinking. But always grinning.

"Then," I took a deep breath and waved at the vibe. "Please enter it."

He nodded and moved, crawled onto the bed on his knees. I thought he was going for the vibrator. That he would do something and 'become one with it.' But instead, he came for me.

He reached out and cupped my cheek. Cradled it.

I felt it.

Not in the visualisation, in my physical body. I could feel someone's palm touching my face and holding it. I gasped and lent into it.

This… no way!

He still grinned as he came forward and touched his lips to mine.

Whatever he was, I was kissing him back.

And feeling it all in my body. The tingles from being so excited and the pleasure from touching and being touched and… *oh god.* "Hmmm," I moaned.

My eyes flickered open and… I was alone. But someone had kissed me. It felt like it… I touched them with my finger tips and wondered; *had it worked?*

Or was that all in my head?

I glanced down to the vibe in it's little nest of rose petals and bit my lip. *What should I do? Do I turn it on and… use it? Would anything be different?*

I was so damn worked up. The dressing up had me part way there, and then the blue man showing up and agreeing! I was ready for some action.

But still, I hesitated.

How was I going to confirm? "Fuck, I need my pendulum," I grumbled and threw my legs over the edge of the bed to go back out to the lounge room to find it again.

This time, I made sure my elbow was resting on my leg and grounded the dangling teabag on the bed before asking my questions. "Is the Blue Man inside my vibrator?"

Yes.

Oh! I couldn't help but grin.

"Does he mean me harm?"

No.

Thank goodness. I wasn't sure what I was going to do if he had lied to me and tried something. Not that I was sure what harm he was capable of doing to me. Could a spirit or entity physically hurt you?

"Can I communicate with him?"

Yes.

"Can he communicate with me?"

Yes.

Oh, well… how?

The yes and no was annoying me. I wanted to know how, wanted more solid answers. But also, was too damn horny to pay attention.

I thanked the pendulum and quickly placed it to the side so I could get to the good stuff.

"Um, hello," I giggled as I picked up the vibe and placed my finger against the tip of the head. "I'm not sure how this is going to work but I would very much like a sign that you are consenting to me using you to… well, fuck myself." I bit my lip.

Why was admitting it out loud so, well, exposing?

My thumb pressed and held the button for the vibrations for the main shaft. Usually, no, always, it started with a steady vibration. No patterns.

This time was different.

I frowned.

Was it trying to communicate through vibes? Was that how we were going to talk? It was impossible for it to have been a fault in the toy itself, it was under a year old and a very, very good brand. No cheap novelty crap here. So it couldn't be a glitch.

I giggled.

"Show me a yes," I requested.

Sharp and repetitive pulses.

"Show me a no," it was just like my pendulum after all. This should be easy to do.

A long drawn-out vibration that slowly dipped off and died. Before repeating itself.

I hadn't pressed the button at all again. It was doing it all on it's own. What kind of witchcraft was this? I knew a bit from when I dabbled but I had never seen anything like this occurring.

"Do you consent to fucking me?"

Sharp and repetitive pulses. I grinned. Talk about enthusiastic consent.

No more preamble, I flopped back and arranged myself. Spread my legs and pulled the crotch of my panties to the side. They were wet. Soaking. *Hmmm,* I really wanted to do this.

I ran the buzzing tip through my lips and circled my clit. The pulsing vibrations made me moan and arch into it more. "Hmm, yes, oh god yes."

Dipping it inside, just the tip, getting it wet and ready. Pulling it out to rub against my clit again. Then plunging it all the way in… *oh shit. Oh FUUUUUCK!* I angled to hit my g-spot head on. The pulsing intensified, like he was really agreeing with this.

I turned on the clit sucker and upped it to 'fuck me' levels. Had to reach up and overhead to grab onto the headboard. Grip hard. Tip my head to the side so my mouth pressed against my bicep and muffle my moans.

I didn't last long.

I screamed, as I came. Clamped down hard on the shaft of the vibe inside. It was too much. I needed it to stop for a moment. I started to pull it out and the vibes changed immediately to the long drawn out no.

Panting I asked. "Do you want to stay inside of me?"

Short and sharp yes.

I whimpered at the over stimulation. "Hold on," I turned off the clit sucker and the main shaft vibrations before pushing it back inside. Seating the sucker firm against my clit. But not causing any more stimulations through vibrations. *Thank God.* If it went too far, I could squirt and that was not a fun thing to clean up.

"Gotta give me a bit to, um, come down from that," I told him.

He buzzed once.

I groaned. "Fuck. Huh, I turned you off… no way," I laughed at it. "That's kind of crazy. I really could give you full control and let you…"

I didn't finish before he pulsed back to life. All areas vibrating on high with direct contact. My toes curled into the sheets. *Oh fuck, oh fuck, oh fuuuuck!* "Oh, oh, oh, oh, ohhhhhhhhh my…. Fuuuuuuuck!" I was forced into another orgasm fast and it left me shuddering and ripping the vibe from me to get away from it.

My body twitched and I laughed as I flopped back. "I did not expect that, ha ha ha."

Still, he certainly had done something that no other being had ever done for me; got me to orgasm in under five minutes. Twice. "Truly, the perfect boyfriend has been created!" I cheered. My fist pumped into the air.

The vibrator still buzzed away as it lay on the sheets.

*

Orgasms.

So many orgasms.

Every night. Multiple times a night.

I may or may not have gone a little cross eyed from it all. But it was so worth it. I felt amazing.

Then, I didn't. "Crap, forgot they were due," I grimaced as cramps attacked. I went about the usual routine for dealing with my period. Hot shower, comfy clothes, pain killers, heating pad, and a nest on the lounge. Snacks, water, tea, pillows, remote, phone. All set.

I snuggled in and distracted myself with rewatching films until my mind wandered. Then I went to social media to scroll until that wasn't doing it and went back to the film. It was a cycle. One that worked. My mind was focused on something outside of my body. I relaxed. It was nice and chill.

I needed the bathroom.

I had to escape the nest and grumble as I shuffled off. While passing the bedroom, I could hear the vibrations.

"What is it?"

The mournful little pulses I'd come to realise were meant to draw my attention grew in their intensity.

I frowned. "Not tonight. I've got my period."

Long and drawn out and dying at the end. No.

"Yeah. I have my period and it sucks and nothing but a period product is going up inside. So, no. Not tonight." I moved on to the bathroom.

The week was long. And the cries of the vibrator were longer. "I cannot sleep with you like this," I complained on the second night. Smacking the lamp on as I reached for it.

He vibrated in excitement, probably thinking I had caved in to his whining and was going to give him what he wanted.

Only I didn't want that. I did not want to do myself while on my period. Did not like the thought of having to clean blood from it afterwards. It wasn't for me.

And he needed to learn.

I stalked to the very other side of the house and shoved him into the linen press. Buried with the stack of blankets I never used anymore so he was muffled. "Calm down. I've already told you that I have my period and I am NOT doing anything sexy while on it. No." Slammed the door and I went back to bed.

Finally, days later, after it was over and I was freed from my monthly cycle, I retrieved the vibrator from his prison.

"I am still not happy with you," I told it. "I am not here as just a hole for you to fuck, okay? I can't do it every day."

It pulsed away, impatient.

I sighed. "Do you understand anything I'm saying?"

*

The book had a scene.

It was similar to the first one, with a suction cup dildo and the chair. But instead of sitting in a somewhat normal manner for sitting on a chair she was straddling it. She'd done that to see the transformation. To confirm her suspicion. As well as, you know, have fun.

I had made an impulse purchase.

It had arrived.

I also had a chair I could use.

Ripping the packaging open, I bit my lip. This was going to be so great. I was going to recreate the scene and get off on it and oh… "Woah… that's bigger than I expected."

My eyes bulged as I took in the huge length and girth of this new toy. Sure, I had seen the measurements in the description when I purchased it. I just hadn't expected it to be so… "Intimidating."

And realistic. Or as realistic looking a cock and balls in a jelly purple could be.

I hummed with anticipation. "Right! Bath time!" One thorough hygiene clean and I was smacking it down to the chair, watching it wobble in place.

The vibrator protested on the other side of the room. "Give it a rest. I couldn't possibly use you for this. I have to use the right tool for the job," and grinned at the current toy in question. "I might need lube, I'm not going to get it all in without some."

And I did need it. I wasn't use to such a size or position. My thighs ached as they held me up so I didn't drop down and sit fully already. Bit by bit, I worked it in and out. Letting myself get use to it, going lower every time. Until… until I sat. "Ohhhhhhhh," I panted. It was a lot of work to get to this and it filled me completely.

How did size queens do this with something bigger?

Was I going to be able to ride this after all? I don't think I have the strength in me to bounce away.

But I needed to move. Not only because I wanted to screw myself, but because it was uncomfortable to be sitting most of my weight down on it. Have it press so hard on my delicate points. And deep.

I lifted my hips and lowered.

"Ahhhh, fuuuu…" I gripped the back of the chair.

Did it a few more times. *Fuck me it was good. I loved it.* It felt like I was getting railed by some dick properly.

But the work was hard.

I had to intersperse it with sitting and rocking back and forth a little before bouncing again.

One hand lifted and played with my breast, squeezed it, pinched my nipple, moved to the other one to do the same.

I wanted to come. I wanted too so bad. But I wasn't getting there from just penetration.

My fingers wandered down and settled over my clit. "Ugh, yes! Yes! Fuck me! Please!"

The vibrator rattled and rattled.

I came.

My head dropped to my forearm as I slowed to a couple of rocks and then lifted off. "Oh god."

Still the vibrator rattled for my attention.

"Hush," I said. "Hush."

Something wasn't right. Something wasn't...

Groggy, I opened my eyes and looked around my dark room. My heart was racing and I felt anxious about... *I don't know.* I couldn't figure out why.

Except, I could feel someone was there.

I could feel them watching me.

Someone was in my home. In my room. They were standing over me and watching me. My eyes gravitated to where I could sense them, beside my bed, right next to my side table.

Oh god. What do I do? How do I fight back? Shit! SHIT! I live alone and I'm a woman and sure I want to fight and live, but what's the bloody chances of me making it out of this? Oh god, I don't want to die. I don't want to be assaulted.

What do I do?!

I took a deep breath... *hold on.*

It was dark, but my eyes were adjusting to it and... I didn't see a person standing there.

But I feel someone there!

I reached over and turned on the light. Sudden brightness flooded the room and made me squint. Sure enough, no-one stood there.

My knees felt week as I moved. Maybe... maybe they were under my bed? Did I dare look? I had heard the horror stories of women going to bed and their killer was waiting under it for them. Do I check? Or do I pretend everything is fine?

What do I do?! Oh god, I don't know!

I did the stupid thing in the horror movies and went and checked. I hung my head over the edge. No-one. Dust bunnies, yes. Intruder, no.

What was going on? I felt like someone was watching me. Like they were standing right there, in fact, I could still feel like a residual energy was hanging in the air.

If it wasn't a human intruder who had broken in, then what the hell was it?!

First, I still had to confirm I was still safe physically in my home. I grabbed my phone and unlocked it, had it ready to call for help if I needed it. Then I got out of bed.

I was shitting bricks. I didn't want to have to check. I wanted to hide and pretend everything was fine.

I went out to the hall and turned the light on. Bathroom light. Lounge room light. Kitchen light. Every room I entered, I turned on the light, checked behind doors, curtains, everywhere.

No broken glass.

Doors were all locked.

Yet, something was in the house with me.

And it was still watching me.

If not human… maybe something spooky?

But why? What the hell was it doing? What did it want? What do I do?

I swallowed hard and straightened my shoulders. This wasn't okay. "Whatever is there, better get out of my house! I am not playing games and you are not welcome!"

My voice carried. "I will kick you out. What does this look like, a hotel? Out!"

I was all bluster. What did I know about banishing things from my house?

All I knew was whatever it was, was setting off my anxiety like crazy. How did I know? Because I had never suffered from anxiety before!

Here I was, heart racing and on edge. I couldn't understand it. I wasn't feeling safe and instead felt like I was being shadowed around my home. And every time I looked over my shoulder there was no-one. But I didn't have to swing my head around to look, because I could feel where they were lurking.

They were creeping on me.

"One, two, three, protected be," I began to chant under my breath. As I did, I visualised a brilliant white light encasing me and settling over me like armour.

The words repeated over and over as I went back to bed. I didn't know what else to do. I was physically safe, I think. Just uneasy as all heck. And this little protection spell should keep me safe.

For a bit.

I turned off the light and closed my eyes.

But he was still there.

Still watching.

And even with my little spell and white light… I didn't feel safe at all.

*

No sleep.

Pretty obvious when I rolled up to sit and dismiss my alarm. I felt like shit. Honestly, no sleep. No matter how much I tried, how many deep breaths I did, and reminding myself that I was fine and it couldn't hurt me physically.

I. Couldn't. Sleep.

The entire time, I was hyper aware of him standing there. Watching.

It was the watching.

It made no sense to me as to why it would want to do that. What was it getting to see? I was sleeping, not doing anything.

I still felt anxious.

I hated it. Never felt like this for such an extended period of time. I had been anxious for things like exams and job interviews. But nothing like this. This was different. Similar, but different. It felt like it was eating me from the inside out.

I was on high alert. Panicky. Heart racing still. Stomach in knots.

Fuck me, I hate this.

But in the morning light, thankfully, I was alone.

Something residual lingered from where it had stood the night before. It seemed to permeate the bedside table... *bedside table?*

No.

What am I doubting? He was the first and only thing that was spooky that I had invited into my house.

And he was on that side.

But why now was he leaving the vibrator to creep on me? Was he doing this to piss me off? To bully me into giving him more attention? What? I seriously had no clue what he wanted or what I needed to do about it all.

Only thing I knew for certain was this was bullshit! I did not agree to this. I had asked if he meant me harm and he had said no. Even the pendulum had confirmed he had meant me no harm.

But meaning no harm didn't necessarily mean that I was safe. Or that whatever he was wasn't creepy.

I hated this. I hated that I needed to get up and get ready for another crappy day at work. Which was going to be worse since I had no real sleep at all. My eyes had been shut, but brain whirring away.

And I didn't have time to sort through things, I had to go.

All day, I was still feeling it. That lingering anxiety. But it was general. Nothing specific could be picked out. Even knowing that it was being caused by some entity lurking inside of my home, it was so obscure and vague. Nothing specific, just overall stressed out and worried.

Getting home in the evening... I didn't want to enter. I stood on the front veranda and fiddled with my keys.

What if he was still there and this didn't stop? What if I stayed in this awful feeling from now on?

God, no wonder people went to doctors for help with this feeling.

Help... I could ask for help.

Now, I hurried inside and locked the door, just in case.

It was still light out, the sun blaring down on all even though it was spring and not summer yet. And I felt nothing when I moved through the house. I went straight to my bedroom and stood in the doorway. Stared at the bedside table.

Only lingering energy. Something dark. It hung in the air and seemed to mark the dresser itself.

But he wasn't out. Wasn't creeping away.

I spun back around and marched to the kitchen for a new teabag. The old one was on the bedside, but if that lingering energy was permeating, I didn't want my pendulum to be affected by it.

Wait... hold on. Sure I believe in all of this, but... well, am I sure? Or is this all in my head? Could this all be just something I'm making up?

What made any of this real?

Even the pendulum. What made the responses I received real? What evidence was there that they were from a higher power? The universe? My spirit guides? Ancestors? Who?! Who was talking to me? Were they talking or was I reading too much into a teabag swinging in the air?

I fretted. Fidgeted with my nails and grimaced. I didn't want to deal with this. I really wanted to go and collapse and pretend everything was fine. Scroll away online or something equally distracting.

But I never felt like this before. I never worried for so long with so much unknown.

The only thing I had was this. Witchcraft got me into this and it was going to help get me out of it.

I went to the bench, plucked a new teabag from the box. Took a calming, or as calming as I could right then, breath. Steadied my elbow. Grounded the teabag before lifting asking my questions to establish my base responses.

It was a new teabag and it felt odd to be using one so fresh.

"Is there something other than me in the house?"

Yes.

"Does it mean me harm?"

No.

Again, that wasn't as comforting any more. I was unnerved and felt on edge. Mean me harm or not, this wasn't how I wanted to live in my house.

"Did I invite it in?"

Yes.

"Is there only one?"

Yes.

I grimaced. That made things easier. And obvious. "Is it the one possessing my vibrator?" I asked to clarify and make sure it was.

Yes.

"But he shouldn't be outside of the toy. What on Earth is he doing stalking me like that around my home?"

No response.

Right, because I didn't ask a yes or no question.

"Can I," I swallowed hard. "Can I bind him to my vibrator so he doesn't creep on my anymore?"

Yes.

I sighed in absolute relief. I can do this. But, how? And there was a little thing of, was it necessary?

"Is he outside of the vibe right now?"

No.

"Will he leave it again?"

Yes.

Ah, yeah it was going to be necessary. I would have to force him to stay inside of it because fuck having a repeat of last night. I do not like feeling this. And he was invited into the vibe for fun. He wasn't given permission to lurk over my bed while I slept.

I thought about what I could do to bind him. There were options, but I was limited if I wanted to have this done quickly.

"Can he leave the vibe during the day?"

No.

"Is he only capable during the night?"

Yes.

Okay. Parameters. Not that those were going to be useful in any way for this. It was just something good to note about the situation.

I chewed my lip and went on the hunt for a notebook and pen. I would also need a permanent marker. I didn't want to do this, but I didn't have much of a choice if this was going to be a repeat of last night.

I brought the pen and paper back to the kitchen bench and sat. Considered what it was that I wanted to achieve. How I would sum it up and word it so it was clear and concise and there were no loopholes to be exploited.

"Are you shitting me, this is more stressful than what dealing with the fae must've been," I muttered.

The back of my neck crawled.

I picked up the pendulum. "Is he behind me?"

No.

"Is there something behind me?"

No.

"Am I being paranoid?"

Yes.

Great. I sighed and scrawled a sentence down fast and sloppy. *Trapped and unable to leave.*

"Is this an intention that will bind the entity to the vibrator?" I asked, hoping it would, just unsure.

Yes.

"Do I need to add anything else or change it?"

No.

Okay. Then I got to work, crossing out the vowels and repeating letters. T R P D N B L V. Hardest part was taking those letters and making them into a sigil. I would find an arrangement that felt like it was proper and then ruin it all by adding the B wrong.

"And this is why people use online generators for this." I muttered. It had been too damn long since I'd done this method. Too many years since I'd last made one and used it. There was a whole double spread in my spell book I had planned out, it was sketched in with pencil, but I'd never inked it up.

Finally, I had a page filled with designs and one was complete. It felt right. I nodded to it in approval. Checking outside to see the sun still there, I went to grab the vibrator.

Once back to the bench, I realised, I didn't want to put him down in a place where I prepared food and ate. No. He was inside a vibrator and that was… eww. Instead, I moved everything back to the bedroom. It only made sense. Everything originated from the bedroom for this.

I set up, reestablished my questions with pendulum and confirmed that he was still inside and unaware of what I was doing.

And then I did it. I took the marker and tested the ink to see if it would stay. It stayed. Strong. Didn't budge when I scrubbed my thumb over it at all.

Excellent.

Then I did it. With a careful hand I drew the sigil, all the while reciting the intention as I did each stroke. Done. I visualised an impenetrable iron casing surrounding the vibrator and sealing it off from everything else. Something that was one solid piece with no gaps moulded to the contours of the vibe.

Trapping him perfectly inside.

Immediately, it buzzed loud and angry. It wasn't the usual flutter of vibrations to get my attention.

I flinched and pulled back. The sun was still out… so he would still be in the vibe anyway, but what if it hadn't worked? What was he going to do to me in retaliation?

I was pissed, too. But that anxiety and worry gnawed away in my chest, making it hard to get a full breath of air.

What if it hadn't worked? What if I'd forgotten a step along the way and messed the whole thing up and he now knows I tried something and he does something back to me? I don't know what to expect anymore.

Was I safe?

Had I done the right thing?

I reached for the pendulum and asked, worry and panic setting in. "Is my sigil working?"

Yes.

Oh.

I didn't allow myself to feel relief just yet. "Can he get out?"

No.

"Am I," I swallowed and tried to say the words needed. "Am I safe?"

Yes.

Okay, that helped. Now I let the relief flood me and I collapsed back into my pillows and sighed. I would be able to sleep again. I wasn't going to have something lurking over me at night, watching me sleep, just being there.

And of course, I had to ask. "Can I still use the vibrator?" Because that was my biggest concern. Jeez, I should roll my eyes at myself. *Why would that be a concern? Why, Heather? You're too damn anxious to relax enough to want to do anything sexual.*

But still… it had been my fave vibe.

The pendulum swung. Yes.

Shit.

I grimaced and realised why. I didn't want to use it anymore. I wanted an excuse to throw it away. Start fresh. New toy. No history. And never invite something in like that ever again.

Because though it had been a hot experience... it hadn't been worth it. He had been more work than a living breathing boyfriend. Yes, easier to get. But I hadn't come into it with the same standards I did when I had been looking for human datable partners. I had accepted the first entity to pop in and agree with my offer and wow...

Did this make me stupid or just really dumb when horny?

I turned to my side and curled in on myself.

Why had I been so desperate to...

He screamed louder with his vibrations. So angry and volatile.

I jerked away from the vibe and abandoned my thoughts. Gratefully. It was going to be a difficult conversation with myself, I knew, and I didn't want to have it. So I was glad to be distracted by the immediate problem.

What was I going to do with him?

"Back to the cupboard you'll go if you don't calm down," I threatened. "I am not having you go off all night. You ruined my sleep last night with creeping and, damn it! Just shut up already!"

I picked it up and shoved it into the drawer, slamming it shut.

He still buzzed like he was screaming away. Like I had betrayed him.

"Fuck you," I yelled back. Anger taking over. "I did not invite you in to be some mouth breather creep watching me sleep! What else were you going to do? Huh? What else was there? Were you going to follow me around? Linger like a shit smell? Fuck you!" I wacked the side table, made it wobble and the things littering it all teetered.

"Now you're trapped. You are never getting out of that stupid vibrator!" I sneered. "You are going to be stuck in it forever! So there! See what you can do to me now, creep!"

And with that I stormed out of the room.

God, please work. Please let my sigil be working and don't let him out at all.

Because if he did, shit, I would be doomed. "This is why we don't fuck around and find out, Heather," I chastised myself. "Because we get into these shitty situations and argh!" I clenched my fists. "You're an idiot! If you'd just been smarter, or not such a loser, you wouldn't be stuck having to deal with a possessed vibrator!"

Never thought I would ever be admitting that out loud in my entire life. Or having to ever use the words 'possessed' and 'vibrator' together.

"Even as a witch you're a failure," I sank onto the lounge and pouted. *Self-loathing. Gotta bloody love it. Ugh.* "This is why you should never have even tried it to begin with. What the hell do you even know about witchcraft? You're not a real one. You can't do real magic. You're just an idiot who thinks she's making things happen. It's all in you're head. Dumb bitch!"

A tear escaped and ran a hot trail over my cheek.

Oh no. Why was I crying? Wasn't I pathetic enough as is?

I sniffled and swiped at the now torrential flood of tears I was bawling with the back of my wrist.

Just perfect. Like I wasn't the perfect little idiot, I had to add in waterworks and make it into a complete dramatic show.

I picked up a cushion from the lounge and hugged it to my chest.

I want... I wanted to be... Ugh! "I don't know what I want. I just don't want to be like this anymore!" I sobbed.

I had been mildly pleased when I went to get ready for bed and found it silent. *Maybe the rechargeable batteries had finally died and he couldn't do shit anymore.*

Or maybe he wasn't inside of it.

"Fuck," I rushed back out to the kitchen for the pendulum to confirm. No, he was still inside, nothing had escaped and my home was empty of anything else. "Oh, then maybe he calmed down," I hoped.

Sleep was fine.

The next morning, I woke up normally and went about my day. It was like nothing had happened.

Same thing that night. And the night after. Everything seemed to be fine.

"Well," I relaxed in bed and pulled up that story on my phone once more. "If I'm no longer being creeped on, then I can go back to enjoying smut and screwing myself silly," I grinned. It was exciting to get back to normal. To also be able to get horny without fear of having something heavy breathing over me and leering.

I returned to the e-book from before. The story was now at the part where he was a real boy and they had to find out if she could accept him for who he is now and not what he was.

"It's still me," he promised her. He was in bed already, sitting propped up with the pillows stacked against the headboard on the right side. The left side, her side, open.

Standing in the doorway she fidgeted with her fingernails. Picked at her cuticles. Still hesitant to take the next step forward.

He sighed, made to get out of the bed. "I'll go to the lounge for the night."

"No!" she jolted forward, her hand coming up to stop him from leaving.

His puppy eyes looked over at her. Was that hope there? Could she see him hoping that she was going to be able to accept that her chair, that had gathered her clothes for her for years, was a living breathing man?

Everything was different.

But he was…

"Stay there," she ordered him. Closed the bedroom door and marched over to her side of the bed. Her face burned. What was she doing? Was she… she was going to snuggle with another person? Not a pile of pillows?

And that person had been a chair before and had watched her sleep in this very bed?

He relaxed back into the bedding. Grinned. "Okay. Only if you're comfortable."

She snorted. "You know I'm not comfortable right now."

He sputtered. "Um…"

She slid out of her dressing gown, dropped that… oh yeah, no chair to drop it onto anymore. Draped it over the foot of the bed and crawled between the sheets. "You've seen what I really am like when comfortable."

His face was red. And he was staring straight ahead refusing to look at her.

She chuckled at his discomfort. "Embarrassed?" she shook his shoulder.

He lifted his arm and hid his eyes behind his wrist. "What do you think?"

She latched onto his elbow, enjoyed that it was a real elbow that she could touch, and tugged on his arm. "I think I should be the one who is embarrassed."

"Why?" he fought her so he could remain hidden.

"Because you saw all of my most intimate and vulnerable moments in here. For years. You know me… but I don't know you." She admitted the last part softly.

And that's when he lowered his wrist from his eyes and looked at her. "There isn't much to know about me," he told her. "And I… um… you shouldn't be embarrassed… I'm sorry I intruded on your privacy!" his face squished tight as he told her that, eyes closing.

Wow.

She liked that he was… well, like this.

That's why she didn't hesitate as she went in to kiss him. Cupped his face in her hands and guided him down so she could reach his lips. It was sweet. Chaste. A little press of lips together.

He froze.

She pulled back. "Sorry," she released his face, hands hanging in the air. "Couldn't resist."

"I liked it," he blurted out.

"Oh."

They stared at each other. Progressively getting redder. Then they broke. They laughed. She leaned into his shoulder to hold herself upright.

He turned his head to laugh into her hair.

"Would you..." she breathed deep to quiet down her giggles. "Like another kiss?"

"Yes, please," he said.

This kiss was not so chaste. Not so innocent. It was lots more movement. He nibbled her bottom lip. She sucked on his tongue.

Somehow, they slipped down the mattress. She laid on her back and he hovered over her on one elbow and his free hand gripped her waist.

She hummed in appreciation and took his wrist to encourage him along.

His hand moved. Slipped under her sleep shirt. Skirted under her breast. Whole palm spanning her ribs with ease.

He broke the kiss. "Are you sure?" he panted.

She gasped for air and tried to think for a moment, completely lost as to what he was asking. "About what?" she demanded.

He chuckled lightly. "The direction this is going."

She hooked her thigh over his hip, heel digging into his ass, and pulled. Ground up into him. Felt how hard he already was. Moaned. Lord, she wanted him.

His hips stuttered and rutted into her. Moaning, he swore. "Fuck."

"Please," she panted. "Do."

Then it was a rush. Fumbling to shove clothes out of the way. Kissing hard. Settling between her thighs and looking down at what he's about to do.

She looked down with him.

Ached for him to do something. "Please," she begged. "I want this. I want you."

He looked back up with dark eyes and through gritted teeth forced out his reply. "Sweetheart, I'm all yours." Reached down, lined himself with her and slowly fed her his cock.

She threw her head back. "Ahhh," as he pressed in. Thighs tightening on either side of his hips. Hands holding onto his shoulders for dear life.

He ducked his head and pressed his lips to her throat. Mouthed at it. Bit. Sucked.

"Move," she begged.

He lifted his head back up and captured her lips. As he did, his hips pulled back, dragging his dick out until the very tip was the only thing left inside.

She clawed his shoulders. Fear suddenly taking over. She whimpered. Wanted to tell him not to pull out.

But she worried for nothing. That slow withdraw was followed by a sharp thrust back in, balls deep, so sudden she was jolted from the impact. "Ah!" escaped her throat.

And then he was repeating. Rutting into her. Pace increasing.

Their kiss became sloppy. Harder to maintain.

Then he was changing tact. Lifted her legs, hooked them over his arms, widened his knees, and… slammed into her.

"AHH! Fuck!" she was screaming now. Toes curling. It felt good.

"Look at me," he demanded.

She didn't realise she had been squeezing her eyes shut so tight. It took another command from him and his pace slowing for her to open them and look.

"Good girl," he dropped a kiss to her lips. "Keep your eyes on me."

She did.

He flicked his hair that was sticking to his forehead out of the way. His muscles flexed with each thrust he made. She marvelled at him. Watched as sweat ran down the side of his throat. Moved without thought and leant up to lick it. Then kissed the skin as he shuddered in her embrace. Bit down. Left her own territorial mark there.

"Stop that," he hissed.

She yanked back, worried.

"I'm going to come if you do that to me."

Oh. She smiled at that. "Come then," she told him.

Shook his head. "Not before you."

She brought her fingers to her mouth, licked them, and put them onto her clitoris. "Hmmm," she whined. Rubbed in time with him.

"Oh fuck," he ground out.

And then her toes were curling. Her muscles clamping down on his cock, wanting to hold him deep inside forever. She yelled.

He grunted, slammed his hips in, deep. Rocked a few times. "Oh shit," he released her legs and lowered himself to lay over her body.

They did it on the bed in missionary. It was hot when he was going to pound town and letting her have it… hmmm.

I squirmed.

Or maybe it was just sex in general that made me all bothered and achy and oh fuck it! I reached over to the drawer and grabbed the first toy that had something I could insert.

And just my luck, it was my old fave and home to a resident creep. "Ugh! Not you, I meant to grab something else…" I pouted as I considered. It was my favourite for a reason. The two ends on it, one long and meant to go inside, and the other shorter and meant to press snuggly to my clit and pulse away. God, I had some of the best orgasms with it.

"Is there any charge left?" I pressed the button.

He roared to life with a strong and steady vibration. It was the standard one, no patterns yet. It shocked me, I hadn't had it act normal since I invited the creep into it. He always communicated through the vibrations and never allowed it to be normal.

"Oh," I pressed the button until I found my old fave pattern. A pulse that steadily vibed away. Buzz, buzz, buzz.

I throbbed, excited to play. Oh boy, this was going to be good. I wanted it. So, I ignored the fact this should be weird and I should probably still be wary of it.

Instead, I shoved my pants down and spread my legs.

"Oh god!" I moaned as I slipped it in, nice and slow and steady, aiming it up to hit my g-spot straight away. "Hmmm, yes." I pulled it back and pushed it in again a few times, writhing on it as I did.

Damn this was good. It was… "Oh, I want more." As I went to press the clit sucker button, the pattern on the shaft changed.

"What? Noooooo," I groaned, disgruntled. *Had I hit the button by accident and changed it?* I cycled through the entire list of patterns until finally I made it back to where I had been.

Only for it to change again.

"No! Stop changing!"

It changed again, only this time, not to a pattern pre-programmed… to a message.

Oh shit. Oh no. What was I doing?! He was still inside and clearly not happy if he was making this difficult for me.

"Please," I tried to reason. "Behave. I just want to cum. I'm sorry that I locked you up in that vibrator. But I needed to be clear that this is what I expected from you when I invited you to possess it. Not the whole lurking and creeping on me thing."

Then the vibe died.

"What is it now?" I pressed the buttons over and over, but to no avail. The vibe was no longer vibing.

I groaned in frustration and collapsed back. Of course, things had to go wrong right as I was horny and desperate to climax. Swapping the vibrator out for another toy was the only other solution.

I fucked myself silly, screaming as I came hard and fast. Oh, that had been unexpected, I thought I was going to take longer to build back up. I laughed lightly, blissed out and giggly. Rolled side to side and grinned. "This," I turned my head to the possessed vibrator. "This is what I wanted. Good vibes and good times."

It remained silent.

I scoffed, rolled my eyes. "Why so quiet now, huh? I don't understand what is that you want from me. I was giving you attention, but noooooo," I whined. "You just had to cut out the power. Well, buddy, you are replaceable."

I shook the toy I'd used in its direction and taunted further. "See here, I have a drawer filled with all kinds of toys that work just fine. I. Do. Not. Need. You. So buck up and stop being a pain in the ass, or I really will get rid of you." With that said, I surged up and carried both toys to the bathroom to clean up.

Did I expect him to start to follow my orders perfectly and be a gentleman from then on? Or was I delusional in thinking I was safe from any retribution that he may bring upon me?

No matter how you looked at it, I didn't bring this upon myself. My expectations were simple and clear, or so I thought. But that aside, I didn't deserve the bullshit to come. What the hell.

*

I was sleeping. Comfortable and peaceful. It was like the previous few nights. Nothing to worry about. Only, I was very aware of my surroundings. I was in my dream bedroom, the one I envisioned when I meditated. My safe space.

I sat up on the bed and looked around. It was like I always visualised… yet it felt different. *What was it?* I couldn't put my finger on it just yet, it seemed to be something just out of reach, but so obviously wrong.

Then he stepped forward.

The Blue Man.

I gasped. "You? What are you doing here?"

He stopped by the post at the end of the bed and lounged against it. He watched me without blinking at all, and still smiling that unsettling and unchanging smile.

I frowned. "Are you the same one that I summoned from before?"

He stared back.

"The one I invited into my vibrator?"

Still, he only stared back at me.

I swallowed hard. *What was going on?* "I thought, um, that is, aren't you bound to the vibrator? How are you outside of it if you are trapped inside?"

Again, nothing but that stare and smile.

My jaw clenched. "Answer me," I snapped. "I don't know what is going on here! Is this a dream?" I hadn't intentionally gone into a meditation and gone to this room. And never in all of the years since I first built this room in my head while in a guided meditation, had I ever visited it in my dream.

But what else could this be?

"Are you angry with me?" I asked.

This time, he moved. He came closer to me, knelt up on the bed and reached out to cup my cheek as he pressed his lips to mine.

I gasped. *Oh...* I guess he wasn't angry then.

Then I was kissing him back. I reached for him, my hands grabbing his shoulders as he moved closer. He started to tip me backwards until I laid on the mattress and he hovered over me.

Oh my. Oh, this was not expected at all... but I was rather enjoying it. Especially as he trailed his hot mouth down my throat, licking and biting.

When he reached the neckline of my sleep shirt, he gripped it and ripped it apart.

I gasped. *Fuck that was hot.*

And then his mouth was on my breasts.

"Uh!" I arched my back to press harder against him, my fingers diving into his hair and holding on tight. I ached. Desperately, I wanted him to hurry up and put something inside of me, fill me up and just, *ugh, just fuck me already.*

I bit my lip hard as he sucked on the nipple, tongue flicking it relentlessly. "Ohhh fuuuck, please. God please!" I begged.

His hands drifted over my waist and to my shorts I had gone to sleep in. These too were destroyed to give him access. And I was overjoyed for it. I never wanted to wear clothes again!

I may even sleep naked from now on if my dreams were going to be just like this. *Yes! Yes!* "Yes!" I panted, his fingers sliding into me and filling me, heel of his palm grinding into my clit, and me writhing on his hand. "Yes!" I threw my head back and moaned.

His mouth released my breast and I cried in pain. "What are you doing?!"

He moved back up, face hovering over mine. The same stare and smile in place.

I didn't know if I should flinch or ignore him. It was unnerving. If I wasn't so riled up and desperate, I'd probably would've had brain cells to realise that this was a bad idea. That letting this entity do me in my sleep was not going to end well.

Except, he curled his fingers as they thrusted in. I closed my eyes, mouth opening wide in a pure pornographic moan.

He took advantage of my open mouth. Shoved his tongue inside and dominated, filled it.

I gasped into it and allowed it. Enjoyed it. Honestly, what was going on? Because this was the best dream I'd ever had.

The last time I'd kissed someone in real life... *when was it? Who was it? Clearly it hadn't been anything of real note if I couldn't recall it.* Didn't care to when this was the hottest thing ever. I clung to him and held him tight so he wouldn't pull away from me again.

But he withdrew his fingers and left me empty. I whimpered around his tongue. *Nooooo! Don't stop! Don't be so cruel to me. Please!*

My hips rolled up on their own, seeking contact with anything. Even if he only gave me a thigh to hump against, it would be more than just satisfactory.

Instead, his hips bared down and... *oh my. Was he... was he always... oh dear god!* I don't think I paid much attention to what was below the waist on this being. His unflinching stare and never-ending smile had held my eyes captive and that was it.

I hadn't even thought about what he could be packing. *And fuuuuck me...* that was no toy.

The blunt head of his cock bumped into me, was being guided to where I desperately wanted him to put it and... and... "Hmmmm!" I moaned as he did enter. A long hard thrust in. Buried deep. Balls deep. *Oh God. Oh shit. Oh. Oh.* "OH!" I broke the kiss to throw my head back.

He dropped his open wet mouth to my throat and worked there to make me lose my mind completely. All while his hips rolled in and out and his dick fucked me.

My nails dug into his back.

It was so much. So much. And I needed him to do more. To nail me like I was nothing but a hole for him and ugh!

Whoa… where had that come from? Since when was I into that sort of shit?

That stray thought was immediately forgotten. Who cared? I was finally getting laid. And it was perfect. Not only was it that overwhelming sort that scratched all of my itches at once. Being filled to the brim, touched all over, not given a chance to think logically. It was also a dream.

All in my head.

I was in control and could stop it any time I wanted by just waking. *But why would I stop?!*

"I want…" I gasped. "I want to be on top!" I demanded.

He said nothing, big surprise. But did comply, his big hands holding my hips as he rolled over and brought me with him. His dick now pushed further as gravity and my weight came down on it directly.

I sat up and rode him.

Placed my hands on his abdomen to steady myself.

My thighs hurt.

But it felt so good. I didn't want to stop. I was chasing my orgasm now, could feel it there, so close, but still too fucking far away for me. *I wanted it to happen now! Immediately. Give me my fucking satisfaction.*

He reached up and cupped my breasts.

Oh! He liked this? My back arched and I pushed them further into his grasp. Stared down at him. Liked it. Liked seeing him spread out under me, his eyes never leaving me. Like I was all he could see. The only one he could focus on.

I grabbed onto the back of his wrists and encouraged him to be rougher. To squeeze, to do more, to touch me how he wanted. Use me.

My speed went faster then slowed and faster again. Never the right amount. Always a little less than what I wanted.

"Fuck," I panted. My face pulled into a frown and I gritted my teeth, hissing through them a I grunted. *Why wasn't I getting there? What was holding me back from reaching my climax?*

What did I need?

I cried. "Please, fuck me!"

With this permission, he wrapped his arms around my waist, pulled my chest down to his, and held me in place. Hard, sharp, and repetitive. His hips pounded up and into me. Fucked just the way I wanted. I moaned right into his ear. Begged him for more. Told him exactly what I wanted. How I needed him to give me more. More. MORE! "YES!" I cried out.

I was so close. It was right there. Right there. Just a little more and I would cum and… and…

My head jerked up. I was groaning.

Another man was there.

What?!

He was like the Blue Man, only red. Eyes staring directly at me. He squatted beside the bed and was eye level with me. And that smile. It was the same bloody smile.

I yelped.

The Blue Man rolled again, putting me on my back. He rutted into me, hitting every one of my nerves perfectly. I was going to cum.

I couldn't stop it. My body felt so good. I was going to cum while this other entity watched me and…

I screamed as I orgasmed. It hit me hard. I clenched down on the cock thrusting inside of me, as if my body wanted to grab on and keep him there and never let him go. My thighs tightened around his hips. I shuddered.

The Blue Man dipped and kissed me again. The same way. Tongue in my mouth, dominating.

I twisted my head to the side to fight him off. "No! Stop!" My eyes flew over to the Red Man. Just beyond him, I could make out dark shadows. More like smudges than shadows, with no solid silhouette at all. They lurked.

And I could feel them there.

Had they… had they been watching the whole time? No. No. No. NO! I didn't agree to this. I didn't want it like this. No!

Wake up! Wake up, Heather!

*

My eyes flew open and I gasped. What?! "No!" I cried out, realisation clear as day. *What the hell happened to me?!*

My body ached. Like I had been railed. Like I had been with someone who had made me cum. The tingles of bliss was still there. But my utter terror overshadowed it.

In my bedside table, he vibrated loudly to get my attention.

The sound hurt my ears.

What did he do to me? In front of... what would they have done if I hadn't woken up? Oh God! Oh shit! I gasped.

The vibrating grated on my last nerve. It rattled and rattled and rattled.

"Argh! STOP!" I roared, ripping the drawer open to pick him up and throw him against the wall on the other side of the room. "SHUT UP! SHUT UP! SHUT UP!"

Tears streamed down my face. I curled in on myself.

I didn't mean to do that. I didn't mean to... it had felt good. I wanted to be held, desired. But I didn't... I didn't agree to more.

I sobbed.

And I hadn't invited more in! I could feel them, the shadowy things that had lurked over the other man's shoulder. They were in my home.

And the Red Man. I shuddered as his eyes flashed in my mind. He wasn't the same as the Blue Man. Yes, they looked the same, and the Blue Man had just... done that to me in front of all his friends. But something was different about the Red Man. He felt like he was more dangerous.

Like he wanted something else from me.

God, what was wrong with me?!

I was an idiot! How could I have allowed that to happen? I'm a fucking slut. A dumb whore. No wonder these creatures were all lining up, I'm so damn easy they could all have a piece of me.

I whimpered into my pillow.

I didn't want that.

This isn't some kinky fantasy. I didn't want to be passed around by all the entities on all the different planes. I was not consenting to this!

I felt violated.

And it had happened in my dream bedroom, my safe space. I had allowed him to do that. Okay, enough of that. Yes, I had been hyped up and all too eager to jump on his metaphysical dick. Yes. That part I knew what I was doing and had enjoyed and agreed to.

I hadn't agreed to others being there. Being watched by them… not knowing what they wanted.

And I most certainly hadn't invited them into my home!

"Get out!" I surged up and glared at the dark, where I knew these pieces of shit were lingering, were watching me from. "Get the FUCK out of my house! You were not invited by me and I will not allow you to stay any longer!"

I didn't want to close my eyes. My skin crawled and I didn't want to have what had just happened play out behind my closed lids, but I needed to. I needed to concentrate and expel these intruders in the fastest way possible.

Banishing and exorcism and cleansing could all be as simple as visualising white light flooding a space and picking up the shit and taking it away. To be incinerated by the light. Or as elaborate as a full ritual, with chants and tools and all kinds of things. Things I didn't have. Nor did I have the memories of how to do them off the top of my head.

But I could visualise.

I could visualise a blinding bright white light pouring from the ceiling over me like a cascading waterfall. Washing me, cleaning away what had happened. Expanding that waterfall to be a storm cloud pouring into my room and flooding it. Sweeping over the floor and under my bed and dragging all of those shadowy figures out. Sending each one to the light.

It grew to include my hallway, bathroom, lounge room, every single room in my house. Until it was pure white light everywhere and everything had been picked up and sent to the light.

Then I thought of the Red Man, thought of him before me and how he leered with his smile. The waterfall fell over him, encircled him, picked him up and lifted him to the light.

I breathed out a sigh in relief.

Had I done it? Was I safe?

I didn't dare check with my pendulum. Instead, I hid under the covers and tried to forget it had happened.

Morning. *Why the Hell was it morning already?* I groaned and rolled over in bed.

Feeling like shit was an understatement. I didn't want to wake up… in a permanent way.

Far out, I hadn't felt like this in years. Hadn't considered how easier things would be if… I just never woke up again…

I swallowed hard.

Oh come on. I was a millennial, we all joked about taking that bath with the forbidden bath bomb otherwise known as a toaster. Offing ourselves as a joke was a generational bonding experience. I mean, what was there to live for? We were dead on the inside and nothing in our lives was exciting or worthwhile. So why not?

Why not just stop existing?

Except, I didn't want to die.

Tears fell.

Ah shit, why did I have to start and feel all self-pitying first thing in the morning? *Ugh, I'm an idiot. A damn lame idiot.*

And a coward. It would be easier, but I just couldn't do it, couldn't commit to the act and end it all. Apparently, I was a masochist and really liked to suffer. Go figure.

I sniffled, scrubbed my hands over my face and groaned.

Now what?

What could I do after last night?

I don't know. I wish I had the answer. I wish that it was something easy to look up. Yet typing in possessed vibrator into a search engine online wouldn't give me the answers I needed.

And I had no-one I could ask.

"I wish I had at least one friend… maybe then…" I trailed off.

Let's be honest, if I had a friend, one, singular, just a friend, I wouldn't have invited a strange entity into my favourite vibrator in the first place. They would've laughed at the idea and called it stupid. I would've agreed and never done it. We'd probably have joked around. And then eaten too much junk food and watched all of the classic films from our childhoods and, yeah. If.

But I didn't have a friend.

Didn't have a coven of witches or a mentor.

Didn't even have a damn houseplant I could go and mope around and talk to.

I was alone.

In the cold light of day, being alone was worse. Night time made me ache to have a lover to hold me. And I could play it off and joke that I didn't need one if I had a battery-operated boyfriend, hell, wasn't that just an upgrade?

But no friends… spending my weekends curled in on myself and feeling like shit. Yeah, morning really sucked.

And the worst of it all, who would believe me?

Shit, would I ever want to admit that something had happened? And wouldn't my own idiocy just be pointed out and I'd be blamed? After all, I'd invited possession.

Had included it in my usual solo play. Hadn't even thought of any possible problems when he'd entered my dream and just rolled over like a slut and opened my legs. What did I expect to happen?

Yet, I still felt violated.

I hadn't consented to his friends being there. To being watched like that. As if just watching they were consuming little parts of me. *Nibble nibble.*

I didn't like how the Red Man had been observing.

I didn't like that he had been there at all.

"I don't ever want to see him again," I hissed angrily. "I hope he disappears and fucks off."

Across the room, as if he heard me, the vibrator started to vibe away. The little annoying buzzing for attention. Whining.

Oh god... that sound made me sick now. I shuddered.

"Shut up," I snapped at it.

It continued.

"I said, shut up!" I surged upright and glared at the thing.

It pulsed away, getting stronger and louder as it did. As if he was yelling back at me.

No! He didn't have the right to do that. I did!

"You will listen to me! I don't care what you think, you do not get to treat me like that ever again! I am not some toy for you to play with in front of all of your friends! And YOU WILL NOT LET THEM IN AGAIN!" I yelled until I was hoarse. "I invited you and that's it! I'm regretting it now," have been for a while. "But I did not invite them and do not accept them into my home and they can all get lost!"

Now he was angry vibrating away. The same way he'd been back when I first bound him to that vibrator…

Which, was that working? If it was working, then how did he get out and enter my dreams? Or, oh god, was he some other entity and the Blue Man was someone completely different.

What the hell had I been doing making invitations to these things? Playing around with something I knew nothing about? Here I am yelling about being treated like a toy, but wasn't that exactly what I'd done to him? Treated him like he was nothing more than a sex toy, to spice it up and make me feel something other than lonely?

I wasn't a witch. I dabbled, like everyone had done so back in the day. But that didn't mean I knew what I was doing or how to fix things! *God, I'm an idiot!*

An idiot who was not going to take this shit lying down. "No," I gritted my teeth. "We are not doing this. I am not doing this!" Surging up and out of bed, I stalked over to the vibe. "You will not get another chance!" Snatching him up, I marched him out of my room and down the hall.

If I thought it would work, I would've thrown him into the garbage bin outside and washed my hands. But I didn't think it would. I didn't know what I needed to do, but I did know that.

So, instead, I shoved him back into the linen press so he couldn't aggravate me with his vibrations. Slammed the door shut.

Think Heather. What do you need to know? You need to know how to seal his ass to that vibe and get rid of it. How to keep him from ever coming back. And maybe how to not be a dumb bitch? Ha.

I rolled my eyes at myself.

Yeah, that last one was a hard lesson I still hadn't learned.

Like any good modern witch though, I went to my phone for help. Searched online for everything that I could think of. Went down rabbit holes I didn't expect. Side tracked. Made notes on things that I could do and searched through the house for anything I could use.

It was a lot.

And I… wasn't sure I could do it.

An idea popped into my head and I seriously considered it. *What if?*

I turned to the pendulum I had left abandoned on the bench and picked it up. "What if I did nothing?" Ah, I couldn't say it like that. *Idiot.* "Could I do nothing? Would everything go back to normal if I did?"

It circled around giving no clear answer to my question.

I chewed on my bottom lip. "Could I stop doing witch-craft?"

Yes.

"And would that fix everything? Could I go back to normal?"

Again, no clear answer. Just cycling through circles and not swinging in any definitive yes or no.

It was frustrating. "But witchcraft got me into this mess, right?"

No. A very clear answer of no.

What? No? But I had used it to summon him into my vibrator. Had used it stupidly. "How the hell is that right?"

I lowered the teabag and considered. *Shit, why was this so hard? I didn't know, okay. I wanted someone to tell me what I had done and how to clean it up so that I was safe again. Why was that so hard to do? Ugh!*

"Do I know the answer?" I lifted the pendulum and allowed it to swing freely.

Yes.

"What the fuck?! Seriously! I don't know! I wish I did and I could fix this already!" Fed up, I tossed the teabag to the side. And stormed away.

Why was I putting so much hope on a damn teabag? It was a teabag. Nothing else. So why? Hell, why did I even care about fixing this up properly? Let's be honest, I am no witch and throwing the vibrator out and ignoring everything else is fucking good enough.

I had never had an issue before and I wasn't using magic all of the time. Why was it that the one time I used it, I had the biggest problem ever? It made no sense. Shouldn't I have been more vulnerable when I didn't have a clue and did nothing?

Or was I so bland that I had to be doing witchcraft to be enticing to some sort of supernatural entity?

I collapsed onto the lounge and sulked.

Whatever. Not like any of this was real. Am I really feeling anything lurking in my house, or was I being paranoid? Was I assaulted last night in my dream or had that been a nightmare? Was any of this real or was it all in my head?

I.

Don't.

Fucking.

Know.

At some point, I must've curled up and closed my eyes. Taken a nap like an emotionally exhausted toddler, knocked out and down for the count. One moment I had been awake and fretting away while glad that the sun was still in the afternoon sky. Then next, I was asleep and dreaming.

Dreaming of what? I couldn't tell you. It was a dream and I knew it was so vivid at the time, but faded so fast once I woke up.

Only, I wasn't awake.

"How did I get here?" I looked around and worried. It was the room. My dream bedroom. And I was sprawled across the heart of the bed. Quickly, I sat up. *This... wasn't a dream anymore, was it?* "Am I really here?"

No, not really. But also, yes. It was confusing. But I did know that it wasn't a dream.

"Am I lucid dreaming?" I got off of the bed and walked around. "I wasn't mediating. I've never heard of anyone waking up in their visualised place before. Oh no. Did I astral project? Is that why I'm messed up? Because my soul isn't properly tethered to my body?" I rambled on with questions and theories and no real damn answers.

Because again, I didn't know.

I walked around the room and considered all of the details. I'd come up with it back when I wanted nothing more than to disappear into the country. Live in a cottage, bake bread each day and read tarot and just be happy. This was what my mind had seen as my dream room. My safe space.

Four poster bed with gauzy curtains. Lots of green. Everything looking aesthetically pleasing and matching. Nothing like the mess I lived in, in reality.

"But it isn't safe here," I muttered. "If it was truly safe then I wouldn't have had the Red Man and the shadowy bitches invading it…" I frowned. *How had they gotten in?*

The Blue Man I had invited… and I assumed he had invited his friends in. But what if I had opened a door and left it open? What if I hadn't done the right thing to begin with and protect my sanctuary and "Oh fuck! I fucked up. Again."

I groaned and buried my face into my hands. Yep. It was so stupidly obvious now that I had been dumb and it was all my fault.

Well, duh!

Who else could be blamed for opening a door into my home? Leaving it wide so that any low vibrational entity could come in and treat it like it was a damn hotel and trash it? Who else? That's right, only me. Because I had done it.

"Why?" I cried. "Why didn't I stop and think properly before going for the most stupid choices?"

And doing no clean up, afterwards. No spiritual hygiene at all. I essentially didn't wash my hands after playing with these things.

"This is why we start with the basics and good spiritual habits, Heather," I scolded. *And,* I thought, *this is why others don't get into the same shit as you do.*

I nearly jumped out of my skin when I felt it. Hands on my waist. Firm grasp, holding me steady. And a body pressing against my back.

My head shot up and I looked over my shoulder.

The wide-eyed stare and that damn unchanging smile… and blue skin. The Blue Man from the vibrator.

"You?!" I yelped. Tried to spin around to face him, only his grip held and I couldn't break away.

My hands slapped away at his. "Let me go! Right now! I said let me go!" Now I was using my nails to claw at his wrists, my elbows to slamming them back into him, my heel to stomping onto his feet and kicking back at his shins.

Still, he held me in place. Pressed every inch of himself against me, I could feel his dick hardening against my lower back.

No! Not this time! Never again! "I said let me go!" I reached over head to start clawing at his eyes. If he never shut them, then I can target them.

A second set of hands grabbed my wrists and pulled them away. Red hands.

Oh no.

I tried not to tremble as I looked forward and saw the Red Man before me. He too stared without blinking and smiled that awful smile. "Let me go!" I demanded. Except my voice was weak. Small. Because I was terrified.

Pendulum had said the Blue Man in my vibrator meant me no harm… but did that include the Red Man? And what did 'harm' mean? Was assaulting me in this room, even if it wasn't where my real body existed, something they considered as not harming me? Was it a loophole to them?

"Please," I begged. "Stop. I don't want this." *I don't want you.*

He terrified me. A massive bulk of a humanoid man and something about him that screamed out of control. I would have no say in what happened with the Red Man. He would do what he wanted to me, regardless of what I wanted. *To him… I was a toy.*

The Blue Man dipped his head and ran his tongue over the side of my neck.

I squirmed, trying to pull away.

"Noooooo!" I complained. Shoulder pinching up to my ear to prevent him from gaining access.

It didn't work. He licked behind my ear, nibbled the shell of it, and sucked the lobe into his mouth.

The Red Man stepped forward and pressed against my front. He towered over me. The same height as the Blue

Man. My hands were kept in his tight grasp as he bent and buried his nose into my hair.

Was he sniffing?

His dick pressed against my stomach. Twitching.

Oh shit. Oh no. No, no, NO!

The hands on my hips lifted and started to stroke me all over. Trailed along my waist, cupped and massaged my breasts, pinched my nipples and rolled them between fingers. I squirmed.

"Stop doing that," I whined.

I hated it… but my body was reacting. And I hated that it was doing that.

But he was using everything I had taught him. Every time I had used the vibrator and touched myself like this. Or the last time when he had fucked me on that bed and I had ordered him to touch me, leaned into it and begged for it to be harder.

Oh shit. I had given all of that away to him. He knew what to do to make my body tingle and beg for more.

Except my brain was screaming a resounding *FUCK OFF!* "No!" I cried and tried to struggle more. Unable to do anything. Sandwiched between these two brutes.

Sickened by the touches, by the smiles, by everything.

Terrified by what was going to happen and all because I had let them in and hadn't been able to get rid of them from my home.

Stupid.

Bad witch.

Idiot.

Witch... My brain caught on that word. On what it meant. I had gotten rid of the Red Man before. Last night. I had also escaped this room last night. This room that I had made and existed for my brain to go into. Where I could change the colour of the walls with just thinking it and visualising it into existence!

I closed my eyes and inhaled.

They pushed on me harder. Kissed my skin, licked, sucked.

Ignore.

Come on Heather. Ignore it and focus.

A brilliant white scalding light beaming down and surrounding the Red Man. Encasing him, picking him up and taking him the fuck away. Sending him to the source of white light to be destroyed. I visualised how his face would be obscured as the light became a thick opacity. How it would feel to have him lifted away. How I could stumble a step forward.

My eyes opened as I did stumble.

I blinked. *Oh.*

Oh my god! It had worked!

The Blue Man grabbed my arm. I swung round with my free hand and slapped his face. "You do not get to touch me ever again!" I yelled. My rage flaring hot with the boost in confidence. *I'd done it. I'd sent the Red Man away and I wasn't going to let the Blue Man escape either.*

Eyes closing again, I repeated it. The light coming down. The way his hand would be removed from me. How it would feel like an empty space with him gone.

And it happened.

I grinned in triumph as I found him gone from my sight. Gone from my space!

Except...

"Ugh, really?" I looked around and sure enough, what I had felt was there. Shadowy little entities hid in the corners of the room, dangled from the ceiling. They now swarmed. They charged at me.

I panicked.

What the fuck?!

"One, two, three, protected be!" I yelled and brought down a tidal wave of blinding white light that picked each one up and encased it in a solid bubble of white and took it away.

Until I was alone in the room.

I dropped to my knees and looked under the bed. Nothing. Checked behind the dresser. Nothing. The curtains. Still nothing.

My heart raced. *Was it over? Was it safe in this room now?*

"Hello?" I called out, listening carefully to the silence. Straining to hear anything that could mean something was there.

I was too hyped up to trust my feeling side, to sense the presence of something else being there.

Was I finally alone?

"What time is it?" I mumbled as I came to on the lounge.

Outside was dark. *Dear god, had I napped that long? Shit.* I hadn't meant to be down like that and unprepared…

I inhaled shakily and sat up.

My skin still crawled as if I had felt them touch my real body and played with me. I shuddered, drew my legs in and hugged my knees.

"What now?" I mumbled.

Well, that was a loaded question. I could sit and sulk and probably face another onslaught of invaders the following night. Since I seemed to be unable to send them away completely. *Or...* "I can get off this couch and do something," I scolded myself.

And yes. I could very well do that.

"First things first. I need to get rid of him," I gritted my teeth. *No, actually first things first I needed to make sure he was bound to that vibrator and couldn't find any loop holes.*

Pendulum.

I set up with the teabag and started with my endless questions. "Is there an entity sealed into my vibrator?"

Yes.

"Does it have a way out?"

Yes.

"Can I seal that way out?"

Yes.

On and on I went. Confirming things I had suspicions on. No more damn theorising or overthinking it.

"Is the entity in my vibrator the Blue Man who attacked me?"

Yes.

"Is the Red Man gone?"

Yes.

"Will he come back?"

Unknown. The little circles around and around made me swallow hard in worry.

"If I set up wards around my house, will that stop him?"

Yes.

Ah! There! There it is and I knew what I needed to do. No more chit chat, it was time to act and to get it done.

"Thank you," I said to the pendulum before dropping it down and swapping it for the notes I'd made during the day. The list of things I could do to protect myself and my space and what I needed for each one.

To the kitchen I raced. Grabbed the empty pasata jar I'd been hoarding with no purpose, along with the empty jam jars. Clearly, I had a problem. But that was a problem for later.

Dug through art supplies in my messy spare room until I found black paint. I applied a thick coat on the inside of the glass jar and lid. Set it aside to dry while I went to get everything else ready.

The sigil had worked but it didn't prevent him from escaping and getting to my dreams and fucking with me there. I needed to be all encompassing with this. Needed to make sure he couldn't find a way out. But if he did, then the jar would be keeping him trapped.

I made a new sigil with the intention of closing off all possible ways out and into this plane and all other planes of reality. Really made sure to emphasise that he was to be bound to the device, after all he entered it on his own and had agreed to it.

He was silent when I retrieved him from the linen press.

I swallowed. Reluctant to touch it at all any more. Jesus. What was I going to do if I was so disgusted with it and unable to finish what I'd started. Teeth clenched, I snatched him up and quickly drew on the sigil and activated it. "You will never leave this device."

Immediately, he started to buzz away in protest.

The sudden vibrations startled me. I jerked and he dropped from my hand to land with a thwack onto the floor.

He stopped vibrating.

Quickly, I scooped him up and dropped him into the jar. Added a scrap bit of paper with yet another intention scrawled onto it, some general items to 'encourage' him to stay in there. And then slapped the lid on and did it up.

Perfect.

Back into the lounge room I hunted around my shelves. "Where did I put it? I know I have an emergency set." Opening random drawers and digging through the contents, I searched all over until I found it.

I lifted it up and into the air in triumph. A candle. Unused, since I hadn't suffered through an electrical blackout in a while. But that just meant I had a full candle of wax.

Mindful of the placement and making sure I didn't set my house on fire, I lit the candle. Poured the melting wax over the lid, sealing the edges. Over and over I poured wax. Thick layer on top of the other thick layer on top of the other thick layer.

The drizzles looked like abstract art.

I grinned at it. "No escape," I said. And turned to extinguish the candle with a puff.

Getting up, I gathered my keys and purse and the jar. There was one last thing to do and… *oh.* I grimaced as I looked outside. Pitch black.

"Um…"

But could it wait until daylight?

I glanced at the jar I was holding in my hand. He was bound to the vibe, the jar cut him off completely. The last thing was to get him out of my house for good and to bury him in a location as far away as logistically possible.

But it was dark. And I was a woman. A woman heading out to a desolate location alone.

Yes, to bury a jar at night, can't get any more witchy than that. And strange. Who buried a jar like this? Though it was a little like burying a body so they couldn't find the evidence.

But it was still night time and I didn't feel at all that confident nor safe taking that step outside of my door.

"Am I being a wuss?" I asked.

Or was I listening to my intuition and not putting myself into a questionable situation?

Hard to say.

"The least I can do," I conceded. Dropped my keys and wallet back down but still went outside to put the jar beside the garbage bins. Then rushed back in and slammed the door shut. Locked it. "He doesn't get to stay inside my house anymore."

I walked back over to my notes and looked them over. Considered what it was I should do first now that he was out of my home for the night. "I'll take him in the morning and bury him," I reassured myself.

Bury him in a place he shouldn't be disturbed.

If I didn't feel weird about it, I probably would've thrown him into the ocean and let him drown. But what if someone caught it and opened it up and found the vibrator inside? A, that would be so weird. B, it would defeat the purpose of sealing him in to begin with. Plus, rubbish in the ocean. *No. Just no.*

My ecco heart would bleed.

"I need to ward my space for the night," I chewed my bottom lip as I considered.

Everything on the list was something that was going to take time and resources. And I hadn't yet settled on one method for protection.

"It just needs to be a quick and dirty. Just for the night. I'll do it properly in the morning," I went to the bathroom to hunt through my cupboards. Surely, I had something I could use.

"Ugh," I grimaced. "Why do I have so much junk in here?" Digging away, right at the back behind some stuff I was pretty sure was out of date and not usable anymore, I honestly hadn't used some of this stuff in over a decade, there was a green bottle with a childproof lid.

"What did I buy this for again?" I pulled out the full bottle of eucalyptus oil. Reading the instructions on the back didn't help. It suggested using it for mopping floors or washing. Do not ingest.

But eucalyptus was good for protection. The properties of it magically meant that it cleansed a space and prevented anything from entering.

I grabbed a cloth and went about the house. Splashing some onto the cloth before rubbing it along the threshold of doors and the bottom sill of windows. Front door, back door, kitchen windows, bedroom. Everywhere.

The smell of eucalyptus invaded the house. It was refreshing, if a little overwhelming. "Smells like a jar of that stuff for coughs mum used to use one me as a kid," I touched my fingers to my chest. Right where she would apply the rub. *Huh...*

Ah shit. I swallowed down the pang in my chest. *No, I didn't have time to deal with emotions from memories. No! Not now.*

Not ever.

I gritted my teeth and finished off what I had started. Then I washed my hands and went back to the pendulum.

"Is my home and I protected?"

Yes.

"How long will it last? One day, tw… oh."

As soon as I started, it swung to say no.

"Not even one day?"

No.

"What about for the night?"

Yes.

Oh.

Oh shit. That worried me. But at least I was protected for the night. It just meant I couldn't rely upon it exclusively. And I would have to do something. Not procrastinate.

If I put it off… well, I did not want to face the Red Man again. I had to do it.

But in the morning. Not tonight.

I sighed. "Is there anyone else in my home right now?"

No.

Oh good.

"Is there anything else I needed to do right now?"

No.

"Can I ward my home tomorrow?"

Yes.

I glanced over at the list and cycled through asking the pendulum what was the best option for me. Maybe it was me being lazy of overly dependent upon someone else deciding, but it helped.

I knew what I was going to do.

And that meant I could go to bed and… stare at the ceiling and flinch anytime I heard something in the night.

Is it them?

Are they back?

Did I mess up again?

The entire time, on edge. Didn't matter that I was exhausted or felt like I wanted to die and be done with it all. I could not rest. I could not relax.

What if... what if... what if?

It all cycled through my head.

My heart raced. "Ah, come on, Heather!" I scolded myself. "You've gotten rid of them for the night at least. The pendulum confirmed that. And you have some sort of protection in place. You can sleep."

I tried breathing exercises. Nice deep belly breath in, hold for a count of four, release, pause for a count of four, and repeat it all.

My heart still raced.

Fuck.

I huddled under my covers and just waited for dawn to come.

When it did, I grumbled and climbed out of bed. My head pounded with a headache. Anxiety was still sitting too damn high for my comfort.

It felt like my body was wound up tight and ready to be startled with whatever it was that attacked next. I hated it. I wanted something to distract me from it. But... well, that's how I got into this mess after all.

I went through the motions of breakfast, even if my stomach tightened into a tiny fist and wanted nothing to be put into it. It would not unclench.

I still ate a little cereal and sipped my tea.

I had messed up because I was distracting myself. Yeah, I had self-awareness when it suited me. When I wanted to acknowledge that I… *hmm, yeah. I am a mess and I know it but I just don't know how to fix it and it all seems too fucking hard to do.*

I stopped eating. Let it sit there and turn to mush in my bowl.

Now what?

"Guess I need to go for that drive," I sighed heavily. Emptied my bowl and rinsed. Found my keys and purse and headed outside.

The jar still sat beside the garbage bins.

I wanted to hiss at it and never touch it again. But I couldn't be free of it just yet if I didn't pick it up and put it into my car. Unfortunately.

On the other side of town, far, far, fucking far away from my home, I pulled into the carpark of the look out. Undisturbed nature grew all around this high point. Usually, the only ones to come out here were those late at night looking to park and make out in their cars.

"This should be the perfect spot then," I climbed out and gathered up everything. Went walking into the scrub. Cursed the first spider web I walked into face first.

Was disgusted to find so much rubbish discarded throughout the undergrowth.

Finally, I stopped and felt like this was the spot. A random location. Perfect for no reason.

I crouched down and used my little garden spade to dig a hole. Went as deep as I could. Spent ages going down.

Cursing the toughened soil. Hating that my arms were so weak.

My headache pulsed away.

I placed the jar into his little grave. "Stay away from me," I commanded and immediately shovelled dirt onto it. Buried it. Scattered the leaf litter anew over the top to hide it and walked away.

Back in the car, I heaved a sigh. Then laughed. "Did I just break-up with my vibrator? Ha!" It was ridiculous.

And yet… I rolled my eyes at myself and headed home once more.

"Ugh…" I stumbled through the door. "It's too early for this," I cried.

But if I put it off, if I sat down and got lost online for a few hours. It'll be a rush to get something in place once again for the night.

Not that I was 100% sure that this was going to work.

I had options. Looking over the list I focussed on the ones that the pendulum had said yes to. Ultimately, the final decision was my own. But it was nice to know I had the right ones there. At least, I hope they are right.

A home guardian. "No," I frowned at that one. "I just got rid of something, I don't want another thing developing into a sentient being and living with me. Sure, it'll be a different dynamic. But too soon." It was simple enough. Choose an item, cleanse it, walk it around the space and talk to it, then set it up on it's little pedestal and have it keep watch. Like a gargoyle. Leave it offerings to keep it happy. But it would eventually absorb enough energy to become sentient and have it's own personality.

And that was a big fat no from me.

Not again.

Elemental warding. "I think this one's a good one… if I have everything for it." I went about and found things; a rock that I'd randomly found outside that just called to me to pick it up. The candle from the night before. A bell. And a sea shell.

"Okay… I think this will work. I should check." Unsure, I asked pendulum to confirm if each item would work, if it was appropriate to use.

Yes.

I still hesitated. It was such a big thing and what if…

I looked back over the list and saw some smaller things I could do. "I have rosemary growing outback." Quickly, I dashed outside to cut some and bring it in. Found some pushpins on my desk and a stool. Went around and stabbed through a spring of rosemary into the wall above every door and window. Going back out to collect more when I ran out. "Rosemary for protection," I said to myself. Explained it like I was trying to teach myself anew about all of this.

A sigil could be next.

That was another easier one to do. "Should I have more than one protection?" I asked the teabag.

Yes.

"Is the rosemary working?"

Yes.

"Should I do a sigil?"

Yes.

I sighed and thought about my intention. How I wanted to be safe in my home and keep things out. Went through the frustration of designing it and then finding something I could draw it on and where to set it up. In fact, I did a couple and placed them over the top of the rosemary on the entryways. Focused on them and visualised them with energy filling them up. Energy coming from a source that was not me, that could be continuously feeding them. The Earth was an obvious choice for it.

"Ugh… I'm exhausted by all this." I collapsed onto the lounge and sighed. But I wasn't finished.

I was tired, but if I stopped…

I didn't want to procrastinate and never get the elements set up and then have a massive hole in my defences.

But I was tired. Exhausted. I was working on no sleep. Emotionally I was a hazard. I was one paper cut away from losing it and throwing a wobbly that a toddler would be proud of.

"I don't want to do this," I pouted. "I just don't want to do anything anymore."

I curled in on myself, arms wrapping around my waist… the closest thing to a hug I'd had in years.

There it was. I bit the bottom of my lip to keep it in, eyes widening so I wouldn't, but it was no use. A sob escaped. Flood gates opened. I bawled. Heaving gasps for air. Snot clogging my nostrils.

And this awful damn feeling of… loneliness.

I was lonely. I didn't speak to anyone unless it was at work.

Shit, work. I hated my job. Hated it yet I couldn't quit because I needed the money.

My life sucked.

I hated it.

I had nothing. No career. No family. No partner. No kids. Nothing that gave my damn life meaning and I just existed for no reason. Got up each day, worked, came home, and doom scroll so I didn't have think about how empty it all was.

No purpose.

I wailed. My chest ached. It hurt. Everything hurt. And I didn't want to feel like this. But... *what could I do? Reach for my phone and find some cat videos to laugh at?*

"You fucking need therapy, Heather!" I scolded myself.

I wished I had someone to talk to. But I had no-one. Not a single person.

So what was the point? What was the point of even trying anymore?

I reached blindly for a tissue on the coffee table. Ended up knocking everything on it to the floor. I cursed and dropped to my knees to pick it all up... teabag included.

I hesitated. An idea half forming as I held the thing up.

"Fuck me, Heather," I snarled. "Are you that desperate that you have to talk to a damn teabag?!"

But I couldn't bring myself to put it down.

What was this? Was I... scared? Why was I scared to ask the pendulum?

I knew that answer. Too well.

"Because I don't want to be told no," I sniffled.

If I never asked, then I never could be rejected.

But I would never be accepted either.

So I asked. "Pendulum… Is my mum there?"

Yes.

I gasped as the tears filled my eyes again. "Can I talk with her?"

Yes.

Oh. Now I couldn't do it, I had to stop and take a breather. Let the tears pass so I could see the teabag's swing.

"Is she alone?"

No.

"Am I alone?"

No.

Finally, I smiled.

Six months later…

"I'm coming," I called out, setting my textbook to the side and made my way to the front entrance. "Hello?" I shivered as the winter wind blew in through the locked security gauze door.

Fuck it was cold.

"Delivery for Heather," the postal worker announced.

"Oh, excellent." Quick fingers unlocked the door and reached out, first to sign for the package and then to take it into hand. "Thank you very much!"

"Have a nice day," they brusquely said and headed back down to the street, shoulders stooped as they went.

I quickly relocked the security gauze and slammed the main door shut. "Brrr, cold! Glad we're inside today. Right, my big baby?" I drifted over to the fat black cat sprawled over the rug right in front of the heater gently heating the room. "You are so spoilt," I squatted and gave them a scratch under the chin.

Purring loudly and lifting their head to give me better access was my reward.

"Spoilt. Spoilt. Spoilt!" I grinned.

They opened their mouth wide to yawn. I withdrew my hand and watched as the cat rolled to their feet, stretched big and long, and then pitter pattered off.

"Spoilt," I repeated once more with a ruthful smirk.

And I wouldn't have it any other way. As soon as I had met the little ball of black fluff crying out for help, I had known that I had to do everything in my power to help.

Four months later and this sassy shadow acted like it had never known what the outside world was like. Fat, warm, a human to clean up the shit they buried in eco-friendly kitty litter, and lots of scritches.

And I was rewarded with their trust and company and on so many occasions, the perfect view of their butthole. That last one was a very unfortunate thing in my opinion. But I was happy with them.

They were a very good kitty. I loved them.

"Right," I pushed myself back upright and headed to the kitchen to find a knife. The package wasn't going to open itself for me… and I wanted in immediately. I had a very good idea as to what it was.

Once it was opened and spread out, I grinned. "Oh my lord! She's perfect!" A box inside another box. The outside box nondescript and a thing to get it here to my hot little hands. The inside box was the product packaging; sleek merchandise photos, a list of features. "Ohhh, water proof. That could be fun."

I opened that box and withdrew the new wand.

A vibrating wand.

"Every witch needs one," I joked with myself.

I looked it over and followed the instructions on how to turn it on. Was surprised it had any sort of charge already.

I chuckled. "Fast delivery and ready to go. It's like they heard someone was horny and answered the call, like superheroes."

But it wasn't ready to go yet. Nope. Not for my hygiene tastes. I gave it a physical clean to make sure all the possible bugs were bye-bye. Then took it in hand and spiritually cleaned it with white light visualisation. Followed it up by doing a little protection spell to ward off any possible bad vibes.

Finally, I popped it onto the charger.

"Just because it has charge at the moment, doesn't mean it will be enough to get me over the line. No bloody way am I having it die part way through," I told myself.

Yes, I wanted to try it out immediately. But I also wanted to see what a full solid charge was going to be like and how long it could last.

Plus, I had chores.

I puttered around. Watered the plants. Tidied up. Made lunch and sat to eat it in peace at the table.

The cat strolled in as I was washing my dishes and twirled around my ankles. "What are you begging attention for? Hmm?" I playfully flicked some water at them. "Attention whore."

A loud meow in protest followed.

I laughed. "Oh really? Is that what you're claiming?" I spoke to them as if they were speaking back to me in English and I understood them.

Obviously, I was very happy to embrace the crazy cat lady lifestyle. Who wouldn't? With such an adorable cat lurking around, it's impossible not to be one.

Once I drained the sink and took off the gloves, I spun around to scoop them up.

They snuggled in under my jaw, bumped their forehead to my chin and purred away.

I cradled them. "Ohhhh, did you want to be treated like a baby? Is that what it was? Come on, let's sit."

On the lounge, I sat and stayed there. Cuddling them. "You are so loved," I told them, giving them a kiss to the head. "So, so loved!" Another big fat kiss.

This time they meowed back at me, as if to say it in return. I idly scratched between their ears. "You came to me when I needed you, didn't you? You knew I needed a cat in my life and found me. Like a little familiar."

I let the constant thrum of purrs fill my chest and… enjoyed it. I didn't feel the need to have to be doing something. Didn't feel the need to check my phone. I was happy sitting there, with my cat, and being.

I wasn't bored.

When the lap cat decided that they'd had enough snuggles, I was released from my duty. And could return back to my text book. I still had half of the assignment to finish before next week, but I'd lost interest in it for the day. "I'll work on it tomorrow," I promised and instead went for a regular book of fiction to read.

This one was exciting and predictable. I really liked how things were playing out for the characters and could guess what was going to happen next. Which was nice.

I liked reading something with a happy ending. Even better when I knew it was going to be happy from the beginning.

I curled into the lounge and read away. Getting lost in the emotions of the characters. Snorted and laughed out loud when they did something funny. Kicked my feet in the air when they were adorable. Grabbed my pencil from the coffee table to scribble down my reactions into the margins of the book. Annotating, but more chaotic.

When I finished the book, I hugged it to my chest and sighed. "Now what?" It was over. And it had been... *whoa.*

Like, really whoa. The sort of story you never wanted to see the end of. When you wanted it to keep going and going. But it had ended. All happily too.

But how was I going to move on from it?

Okay, I'll admit, the lingering need to scroll online or watch a few videos called out to me as I lay there. I didn't have the capacity to jump straight into a new story, but I didn't want to wallow in this one non-stop. "God, I hate the book hangover." And this one was going to be big. It was a good book.

Really good.

To the point that I wanted to tell everyone all about it and make them read it so I could have people to talk to about it.

But, I only had my cat.

And they were a good listener on the whole when they wanted to be. Not so good with discussing the finer points.

Friends were still something that was taking time for me to make. Real friends. Not shallow ones.

"Maybe I could join a book club," I wondered out loud.

I shook my head. "That might be after my exams. Not enough time for that at all."

I did indulge and pick up my phone. My social media that I scrolled through was curated. It showed me books, cats, witchy things, holistic, and lots of nature shots. Oh, and plants. Couldn't forget the plethora of plant babies I was watching online.

Fifteen minutes was all I allowed. And all I needed. I recognised immediately when I was zoning out and doom scrolling and quickly turned it off and sat up. Arms stretched over head. I leant this way and that into the pull of my muscles. "Hmm." I released my arms and flopped down.

"I wonder if the wand is charged?"

When I checked, the light on the side was a steady glow. "Excellent," I grinned. Excited to test this new toy out.

Since 'the incident' I was a little more cautious of sex toys. Not that I expected one to be possessed all on it's own or that I was going to suddenly open invite to anything again. No. It was something like trauma, I was still processing it and unsure of how to view it.

Shadow work in my journal was helping. But it was slow.

I was restricted to my fingers, a pile of pillows or just a dildo when masturbating. Vibrations left me… panicky.

Not that I wanted to be afraid. But it reminded me every time of the Blue Man and the Red Man and… well,

I felt awful and shameful. Because I had brought it upon myself.

"Unknowingly," I reminded myself. "It was an accident. And you're allowed to make mistakes. Learn from it and move forward," I gave myself a hug and allowed the emotions to flow through me. The hurt and guilt and shame, but also, the excitement.

I still loved masturbating.

Loved the way it made me feel. Obviously, I felt good when I orgasmed. That was a no brainer. But I liked how I felt leading up to it, the anticipation as I sat around horny. Knowing I was going to finger myself silly real soon. The sensation of touching myself, how every nerve ending bloomed and then the build up to orgasm. Until finally, it all broke and I came.

Fingers were good, they were versatile. Inside, outside, one finger, two fingers, three fingers. And then there was a second hand and that made things… open up.

A dildo could do things, but a little less than fingers. A lot less. Still, the feeling of being stuffed and filled was enjoyable at times.

Pillows were difficult and time consuming. That was more about the journey than simply reaching an orgasm. I would stack three on top of each other and wedge them between my legs. Ensuring my labia was opened and my clit, through my underwear, was in direct contact with the top pillow. Then I would ride. It hurt my thighs and hips to be doing it, but fuck, it was fun. I liked rolling my hips and dragging my clit back and forth, back and forth, back and forth. Hands gripping my headboard. When I would finally reach my peak, I would be so edgy and begging to cum. But it wouldn't be anything amazing and explosive.

A little orgasm.

A little death.

But I still liked it and would indulge whenever the mood struck.

I liked to feel good. That hadn't changed at all. It was a fear of the vibrations. An association with the Blue and Red Men and I hated that.

"No more fear," I reassured myself. "But," I sat on the edge of my bed as I psyched myself up. "It's okay if I fail this time. If I have to stop. It's okay. You are safe, Heather." I placed my hand over my heart and tapped it. Solid, firm taps the same way you would tap a baby's back to sooth them as they whinged. "You are safe and pro-tected."

Deep breaths.

Right. I considered the new toy and grinned. Time to get started.

I stripped off my clothes. Instead of jumping into bed and spreading my legs as wide as I could, I took my time. Watched myself in the mirror. Admired the curve of my hips and dip of my waist. My breasts were lower than they had been ten years ago. I grazed my hands over them before cupping and massaging. Still very nice breasts.

Tilting my hips, *fuck me,* my ass came into view. Still an amazing ass. Something to be proud of and to smack. I did that, gave into the impulse and gave it a sharp smack and giggled like a fool for doing so.

I rolled my eyes at myself, but then fought the bad habit of calling myself stupid. Degrading myself. *No. There was no need to call myself an idiot.*

I am not an idiot. I am not stupid. And I am allowed to enjoy my body and things that make me laugh that could be considered foolish to other people.

I do not have to chastise myself… Instead, I scold myself into being more kind. What an oxymoron.

I chuckled and lay down on my back, pillows propping my head and shoulders up. And reached for the toy.

"Okay," I breathed out slow and controlled. "Just a little bit," I reassured.

Turning it on with the button on the side, I nearly jumped out of my skin in surprise. "Oh my!" A strong vibration even on the very first setting. I smirked. Charging it up had been the best call after all.

"Hmm," I squeezed my thighs together. Could already feel that anticipation throbbing in my clit.

I cycled through the list of vibrations, to see what could be on offer. Low, medium, high. And then… patterns.

I turned it off as soon as I felt the pulse going into some pattern and placed it to the side.

Oh fuck. That was… to similar. I swallowed hard and took my time to adjust.

"It's similar, not the same," I reassured. "At least the steady vibrations didn't cause a reaction."

A win and a loss. I did rather like patterns, certain ones low key mimicked the feel of being nailed.

"I can work with this," I promised myself. "I can work with this and still feel good. I will not let them take this away from me!" Again, I picked up the wand and pressed it on to the very first setting of vibration. Low.

A steady, uninterrupted thrum. I placed it on my palm. It was powerful. Traced it along the inside of my wrist and squirmed under the intensity. "Ah!" I started to giggle. Over my body, I dragged the bulbous head of the wand. Collarbones. Down along my breasts, traced around each one and rubbed over my nipples. I bit my lip hard.

Shit, that was good.

Over my belly made me laugh. Either side of my waist, up and down.

My hips.

The closer I got, the more my clit ached for the contact to come.

Thighs.

Yes, I was detouring and being a tease. But the build-up was intoxicating. I wanted to drown in this overwhelming feel of sensations. God, it was good.

Inner thigh. That crease where thigh and hip met.

Outer labia.

"Ohhhhh," I hummed high in my throat.

That was strong. I could feel it vibrating along the lip and up and over my covered clit. *Shit. I don't think I'm going to last very long with this toy.*

Shifted to the other lip.

Then lower and pressed it between both lips, pressed it and rubbed it to get it wet and… and… "Hmmmmm, fuuuuuuuck me!" I cursed.

Unable to hold back and tease myself any longer, I dragged it right up between my inner labia. Brought it directly to my tensed aching bundle of nerves. My clitoris.

I sobbed. Unexpected. *Oh shit. Oh god. Please! Fuck!*

My toes curled, heels dug into the sheets and I held the handle in a tight grip.

"Hmmm," I whined. I whined and writhed on the toy and let the pressure build and build and build, wanting more. Wanting it to be doing more than going at such a low fucking hum!

My thumb pressed on the button to increase it. The bump up from low to medium, shit. My ass tightened with my thighs and lifted off of the bed. Then dropped fast when that pressed it too hard to the new vibrations.

Ahhh! Too much too soon!

I rode the toy with slow thrusts up, chasing the end, loving getting there.

Panting, I took it to the last of the steady vibrations and pulled it off slightly, a little adjustment. Didn't want to make my clit go completely numb. On and off I pressed. Over and over.

Until…

"OH GOD!" I yelled. Thrashed about the sheets. Yanked the wand from my clit and shuddered. A giggle came out next as I relaxed into this blissed out state.

"Ah, oh my. That was," I gasped for air. "That was fun," I laughed. My thumb turned off the toy and I rolled away from it to smother my giggles into the pillow. Lord, if I wasn't trying to get my life into order and live it instead of just existing, I could be tempted to allow myself to get addicted.

Surely, I could find a way to fund my life from being addicted to orgasming from a vibrator. There were entire categories on porn sites dedicated to the stuff… yes, I knew about them! Frequented them over the years.

Never made content myself. But now… if I could turn something I loved to do into a day job and could spend all day doing it…

Very tempting.

I rolled my eyes. Yeah. Tempted. I'll add it to my list of things I want to do in my life time. Make my living masturbating. Right alongside of finishing my schooling and building my career. You know, the other one that I've started working towards? Not enough time in the day.

But in another life, maybe…

"Not called a magic wand for nothing," I snorted. And I bet that it was a record time for me. "Even with a warm up, that shouldn't have been longer than seven minutes, surely."

Seven minutes in heaven.

Oh dear, it seems my brain has gone to mush after that. I laughed. And laughed. And ended in a hiccup of a giggle.

Rolling onto my back once more, I took stock of it all. How did I feel? Damn good. But it wasn't just the orgasm.

Other than that one little mishap with the patterns… I didn't seem to be affected so much anymore. At least, I was handling it better.

Didn't feel anything negative lingering. No shame or fear or paranoia. Only felt like… I kind of wanted to have another go.

I snorted and kicked my feet and rolled and squirmed and then released my little squeal of delight. "Heather," I chastised. "Give yourself enough time to breathe and recover before going in for another round."

Yes, of course I was going to be responsible.

I got up, nearly collapsed back down with how sensitive I was, just closing my legs together rubbed my clit. *Fuck me. No! Need to…*

I glanced back down. Smirked. "Fuck it," I dropped back onto the bed. I could be a responsible witch after I'd had another orgasm. Or six.

Hello,

Thank you for reading. I hope you enjoyed A Witch's Wand.
I would much appreciate it if you did leave an honest review wherever you like to leave reviews.
If you would like to read more head to
aprilklasenbooks.weebly.com
Happy reading,
April

Author Bio

Independently published author. Artist. BL and fanfic whore. April Klasen lives in regional NSW Australia. Find her @defiantdame on most social media sites. Or sign up for the book newsletter at her website aprilklasenbooks.weebly.com. More books are coming.

Also by April Klasen

Blair: Salem's Daughter
Blair: The Sleeping Daughter
Blair: The Same Daughter
The Annual
Beta
Pure PopAsia
I Heart PopAsia
Summertime Madness
Hook-up or Date
Fitz: A Queer Pride & Prejudice Retelling
A Witch's Wand

9 781923 217997